The curse of thirteen

By

Perry Pankratz

Perry Pankratz

The Curse of Thirteen is a work of fiction. Names, places, events, or other inciting events, Deities/martyrs, are from the creative mind of Perry. Pankratz, and are used fictitiously. Character Amanda Jay's image is actually, Brittany Losonsky-Prentice, used with permission(s). Any other resemblances to actual persons, living or dead, events or locales are coincidental.

Copyright © 2018 Perry Pankratz

Published in the United States by Lulu.com
LIBRARY AND ARCHEIVES CANADA CATALOGING-IN-PUBLICATION DATA
Pankratz, Perry (Perry P.)
The Curse of Thirteen/Perry Pankratz

ISBN 978-1-9994821-2-1

Printed in the United States of America

Lulu.com

First Edition

Book cover design, Zoe Hudon

<u>Dedications</u>

To my loving wife, Teresa… no matter where time takes us, and if I find myself lost in the wastelands of the unknown, I'll find my way back to you. Together we are one… alone, I'm nothing but lost. Thank you for standing with me.

Brittany Losonsky-Prentice, a big thank you for allowing me to use your image for Amanda Jay. I hope you know how much I respect you as a friend.

Sam Stinn, an editor with a true gift for the written words. I'm glad I found you in my dark times as you turn my words into light… thank you!

Zoe Hudon, a great artist. I admire your ability to draw what I see in my mind. Thank you for being a good friend, and an artist I can count on… thank you!

Brittany Losonsky-Prentice

Perry Pankratz

Index   Page

The curse of 13

June 1, 1999

Looking at the clock, it's three forty-eight p.m. I walk out of my office and head down the hall, stopping to knock on room 14's door.

"Hello? Mr. Noble? Check out time is 11 a.m. I've tried calling eleven times," I call out, agitated.

I listen for a response as I'm reach for my master pass and slide it across the reader. It clicks, and the door is unlocked. Entering the room, it appears as if no one is here. The only possessions in the apartment are two suitcases and an overnight bag with Ted Noble's name on it. Walking through the room, I look for any sign of Mr. Noble, but find nothing. Walking into the bathroom, everything looks right until I see the gray sandy substance in the shower.

"Damn... will people stop leaving the shower like this? It looks like housekeeping will be coming to clean it up," I mutter angrily as I grab the suitcases and bag on my way out of the room. Walking up to the desk, I ask, "Excuse me, Vanessa, would you call housekeeping and get them to clean up room 14? Mr. Noble left a mess in there."

Vanessa looks serious as she picks up the phone and replies, "of course, Mr. Harding. I'll call right away."

"Thank you, I am just going to take the bags down to the storage room. I'll be back shortly."

I get to the storage room, put the bags down, and grab my key card to open the door. I flick on the light, and notice the room is packed with luggage. Walking through, counting, there are over a hundred suitcases. I place the three bags near the door as I expect Ted Noble will return for his luggage. Once I get back in the office, I'll have to put Ted's name and a number of these items into the logbook. After logging everything in and placing the book on the shelf, I take a sip of water, and check over the numbers before I am done for the day. A knock on the door interrupts me.

"Come in!" I exclaim, happily.

Amanda walks in and asks. "Excuse me, Mr. Harding."

"Hello, Amanda, you're here a little early. What can I do for you?"

She tosses her hair slightly to the side as she explains, "I just received this message from Mrs. Noble. She was wondering if her husband is still here? I don't have him checked out, so I told her yes."

"Yes, that's okay, Amanda. When Mr. Noble shows up, his bags are in the storage room in the basement. We are also going to add a cleaning fee; he left a mess in the shower. He probably just had too good of a time in our fair city. I'm sure once he's had enough of Saskatoon he'll be back to claim his luggage," I answer happily.

As she smiles back at me, I think to myself, "*I'd love to run my hands through her soft brown hair when it's not in a bun and look into those gorgeous green eyes and lick off that sweet scent of vanilla perfume ... how did God put such a perfect package together in that 140 lb. 5'9" frame? I'll never know, but I want some."*

Amanda gives me an uncomfortable smile and assures me, "yes, I'm sure he will. That was room 14?"

"Huh? Oh, yes. I don't know why people insist on bringing sand into that room. Thank you for letting me know, I'll write a note that his wife called. Oh, since you are here early, perhaps I will leave early if you are willing to start early?" I ask.

"Yes, of course. I'm here anyway so I might as well start."

"Thank you, I appreciate that. I've had a headache all day and it's driving me crazy. If you need anything, all the numbers are right here." I state.

Amanda smiles, and nods, "Yes, thank you, Mr. Harding. I hope your headache goes away."

I grin as I answer, "Just call me Josh. And yes, I'm sure it will." I continue, thinking to myself, *"it will as soon as you quit running over my mind so much it will."*

"I will do my best to keep everything in order. Are you all right, Josh? You look a little flushed."

"Yes, I'm fine. You'll be fine, too; the night shift is fairly straightforward."

"Okay, I'll see you in the morning, Josh."

"Yes, hopefully I can shake this thing. It feels like someone is stomping on my brain… anyway, I'll see you in the morning," I reply, again thinking afterwards. *"Shit! I'll have to wait until she leaves… Wait! I'll ask her to grab my briefcase."* Am

"Yes, have a better night, Mr. Harding…I mean Josh."

"Huh? Oh, yes. I plan too. Please let me know if you have any questions. I know when I first started as manager I screwed up, but I don't think you should have any problems. If you do, please call me right away. Would you be able to grab my briefcase over there for me please?" I ask.

"Sure? I will, but I'm sure you taught me all I need to know."

As Amanda passes me my briefcase and I place it in front of me, I respond, "I know, I was shocked at how fast you picked up on everything."

"I guess it helps when you pay attention to what someone is showing you."

She gives me a somewhat knowing look as I stand up, keeping the briefcase firmly in front of me. "Yes, that is true, Amanda, but I'm going get out of here before I'm needed for something. Thank you again and have a good shift." I exclaim, hurriedly.

As I leave the room, I think to myself, *"now, for a change of pants."*

That's strange?

A young couple walks up to the front desk smiling and happy as they snuggle close to each other. The man leans against the woman, a warm glow surrounding their faces, and asks, "Hi, we'd like a room for the night please."

"Okay, do you have a reservation?" I reply, smiling.

He frowns a little and states, "no. I'm sorry, we don't."

"Well, let me see what we have here... we have room 14 available if you'd like that? I'll need to see your driver's license first, please." I respond, watching as he pulls out his wallet to pick out his driver's license. "And how will you be paying sir?"

He passes me his license as he replies, "credit card. I can't believe our car broke down, we just got it fixed last week."

"Thank you. Sometimes unexpected things happen, Mr. Johnson." I reply. They both nod, and the woman cuddles closer.

"Yes, they do. I just wish it wouldn't happen, every time we're in a hurry to get somewhere ha-ha."

"That's the chaos theory at work for you. I've had many of those myself, Mr. Johnson. Here's your credit card back, and here's your key card to room 14," I reply, pointing down the hallway.

I watch them holding each other and can't help thinking, *"what I wouldn't give for that kind of love."*

They stop, just before they pass the first door, and the man turns and shouts back, "thank you! And your name is?"

"Amanda Jay, but you can call me Amanda," I exclaim, happily smiling at them both.

"Thank you, Amanda. Is there anything open where we can grab a bite to eat?" He asks as they come walking back to the desk.

"Yes, depending on what you want to eat. There's a McDonald's within walking distance, or there is a fancier dining place about seven blocks away." I explain.

"So, honey? What'll it be tonight? Do you want a burger and fries at McDonald's, or do you want to go for a long walk and have a classy dinner?" Mr. Johnson asks, turning to his wife.

"Let's go for a long walk."

"Okay, your room is just down the hall there. You have yourselves an enjoyable evening." I exclaim, smiling.

Watching them walk down the hall together brings a smile to my face. As I click all of their information into the computer, I notice three of the corridor lights start flickering as they go by. I pick up the phone and call maintenance to get them up to check it out.

As I finish putting the last item in, they come walking back to the lobby. Mr. Johnson has a sour look on his face as he asks, "excuse me, Amanda, can I bother you for one moment?"

"Yes, that's what I'm here for. What can I help you with?" I reply, curiously.

He seems nervous as he states, "when we went to the room, it smells like something rotten."

"Rotten? Edna in housekeeping never mentioned anything about that; I'll get them up here to redo the room for you. I am so sorry about that," I respond, appalled by the thought.

"It happens. As long as I don't have to sleep with that smell, I'll be happy."

"I assure you, Mr. Johnson, they will take care of it right away," I reply, hoping this doesn't get back to Mr. Harding.

"Thank you. We'll be back in a couple of hours. Should I leave my key card here for you?"

"No, that's fine, Mr. Johnson. They have a passkey. I assure you that rotten smell will not be there when you get back. Even if I have to take care of it myself." I explain, trying to smile.

Picking up the phone, I get a hold of housekeeping and ask them to come up to the front desk immediately. Thinking about that smell he described makes me want to puke. After fifteen minutes housekeeping finally, arrives.

"Did you not clean room 14 this morning?" I ask, sternly, thinking, *"I hope this wasn't on purpose."*

Edna looks at me confused, and explains, "yes, Miss. Jay, we did. We did it at 9:14 this morning. Someone reported a cracked end table and we changed it, but that was the only complaint with the room. Why? What's wrong?

"Well the people I just put in fourteen complained of a smell. They said it smelled of something rotten in the room. Could you please go check and remove any odors that may be there, Edna?" I ask, trying to hold back my anger.

"Yes, Miss Jay. I will go in there personally and clean the room myself."

"Thank you, Edna, You're the brdy."

I watch Edna go down the hall, past the technicians checking the lights. They start to flicker as Edna walks past them, and stop after she has passed by. The men come up to the front desk about 5 minutes later.

"I'm sorry, Miss Jay, there's nothing wrong with the lights. Even when Edna walked by, there was no power surge. I don't know what to tell you," Kalvin states.

"It's just one of those days I guess," I exclaim, dumbfounded.

I think to myself, *"of course this is happening on my first night as manager… is a car coming through the front doors next?"*

"If it happens again, let me know and I'll keep trying to work on it," Kalvin interrupts my thoughts.

"I will. Is Edna still in room 14?" I ask, curiously.

"I believe she is… she hasn't come out of there yet that I've seen."

"Okay, thank you. I'll go check on her."

I watch the maintenance men head back to their office before I walk around the counter and start towards room 14. I pass the lights that were flickering before, and get a feeling in my insides. The closer I get to the room, the worse I feel. When I finally do get to the door, I knock twice but there is no answer.

"Edna? Open the door please."

There is still no answer, so I pull my key card out and slowly slide it across the lock until I hear a click. I open the door slowly. The room is dark and scary.

"Edna... Edna? Are you here?" I whisper, quietly.

Light from the hallway slowly shines a beam of light across the floor, then the bed, and then the wall as I push the door open all the way. Stepping inside, I try to turn the lights on, but nothing happens as I click up and down on the switch. A disgusting smell wafts across my nose.

"Oh god in Heaven , what the hell is that smell? That's a rotten smell. Edna... Edna are you in here?" I exclaim, gagging.

I listen for a sound, but can hear nothing but the traffic outside. I creep a little further inside the room and Edna's voice catches me off-guard.

"Excuse me, Miss Jay."

My heart beats in my chest like a drum from fright. I try to regain my composure, turning towards Edna, who is in the hallway by the door.

"You scared me half to death, Edna. Where were you hiding?" I shout.

Edna looks at me confused as she replies, "what do you mean where was I? I was looking for you. I started cleaning the room and then you called me. I couldn't find you, so I went and grabbed the industrial cleaner before coming back here. I just had a feeling you were in room 14."

"I didn't call you, Edna. I just wanted to see how it was coming with the cleaning, so I came in here to look for you. You said I called you? Did you see me?" I ask, confused.

"No Miss. Jay, you said it through the door."

"Through the door? This is the first time I came this way. Are you sure you didn't hear the technicians talking?" I ask, still trying to figure out what's going on.

"I may have, but I was sure it was your voice I heard. It probably was the technicians, though. I'm sorry, Miss. Jay, I'll get right on cleaning this room."

"You didn't notice that smell this morning? It is quite bad," I exclaim, trying not to gag again.

Edna nods, "they cleaned the room before I came on shift. I'll start checking on their work from now on, Miss. Jay."

"Yes, do make sure they are cleaning the rooms. I'll talk to Mr. Harding, and see what we can do on our end to help you out," I reply, smiling, but still bewildered by the smell.

"Thank you, Miss Jay. Any help you can give us would be appreciated. I'll get to cleaning before they come back."

"Okay Edna, let me know if that smell is gone in the next 20 minutes. I may put Mr. Johnson and his wife in another room if not," I affirm, hoping she will have that smell gone.

"Yes Miss Jay, I'll let you know."

I think to myself, *"I hope she can remove it, otherwise I will be suggesting we burn that room!"*

Quickly stepping away from the room, I head back to the front desk, looking back a couple of times just to make sure nothing was following me. Back at the desk, I occasionally look down the hallway.

Edna comes walking down the hall towards the reception area. She stops and states, "Miss Jay, that smell is still there. Do you want me to continue cleaning?"

"Yes, if you don't mind. I'll find another room to put Mr. Johnson in. Do you know what that smell is? To me it smells like a garbage dump," I exclaim, grossed out.

Edna looks at her feet, then up at me and whispers, "to be honest, it feels more like a curse to me."

"A CURSE? What kind? I am not familiar with curses," I answer, taken aback.

"Yes, Miss. Jay. Back where I came from, people practiced dark arts or Voodoo. I know it sounds crazy, but back home people used to believe in this. A large number of individuals used to say, including the priests, the spirit worlds belong to a massive universe of their own. Spirits mingle among themselves, but other times they want back into this world. I know my mama, God rest her soul, said never disrespect the dead. She also said the dead have a significant number of powers unknown to us. She said that when she was younger she made that mistake and accidentally stepped on a grave."

Suddenly a loud bang interrupts us. Turning to look, we see Jerry picking up a pan off the floor.

"You okay there, Jerry?" I ask, watching him pick up the pan.

"Yes, thank you, Miss Jay."

"Okay… Go on Edna." I reply, turning my attention back to Edna as she takes a breath and continues.

"Where was I? Oh yes, my mother said that until she reached the age of thirteen, the spirit of the man who was buried there haunted her every Friday. She took gifts to the grave, flowers, candy, and even money, to make up for the deed she had done. When she was thirteen, a man came through town and stopped, asking to see her. My mom told him about the man who was haunting her every Friday at the time she stepped on his grave. 1:39 p.m."

"Hang on a second, Edna," I exclaim, grabbing a piece of paper coming through the fax.

"The stranger asked my mother if she knew why the man was haunting her, and she said she didn't know exactly. Then the man explained to her that thirteen was a complex number in the spirit world, and that the number represented a door to this world. He told my mother these doors could create openings from our side. The number thirteen in our indulgence opened their side and enabled them to come through. He said once they were through, they could cause mass havoc on the souls of anyone who annoyed them. The man and my mother went to the graveyard she had stepped on those many years ago, and they both knelt down at the foot of the grave. The man said some words, and then asked my mother to hold out her left hand, palm up. He stuck a pin through my mom's palm, and as the blood oozed down onto the man's grave, they both said a prayer. My mother said afterwards the spirit never haunted her again."

"Edna, is that a real story?" I ask pessimistically.

"I can't say, Miss Jay. My mother did show me the scar on her hand from where she said the man poked her with the pin. Can I say that it is all true? No, I can't say that. It might be folklore, or it could be the truth, it all depends on your belief and the spirit world I guess."

"Where were you born Edna?" I ask, thinking that her answer would be Haiti.

"Romania originally. Mom lived in Haiti, and we moved to Canada when I was eight years old. Poppa and mother said they moved to make a better life for all of us. I don't remember too much about our home there. I know my parents never spoke about Romania or Haitian once they were here."

"I'm sorry for intruding so much into your childhood," I reply, feeling bad.

"That's no problem, Miss Jay."

"Please, call me Amanda, Edna," I ask, trying to be friendly.

"Okay, Amanda."

"So how did this man haunt your mother?" I ask, still curious.

"Well, mother said that he would stand in front of her, and if she tried to go around him he would trip her and make her fall. Then he would whisper in her ear. Mama never told me what he whispered, but mother said that it wasn't anything good."

"Do you think that's what we have going on in room 14?" I ask, skeptical.

Edna shrugs her shoulders and replies, "I can't say for sure that's what's going on in there, but there's something strange about that area. Last week, when I was cleaning up in there, I got the feeling someone or something was watching me. Nothing bad, just that feeling you get when someone stares at you."

"I get that feeling as well. I'll be standing at the desk here and then out of nowhere I just get instant shakes. You know, like someone pouring cold water down your back," I exclaim, shivering.

"Yes, I know that feeling you're talking about. I usually get it when I go visit my mother's grave. Something about that particular room gives me the chills, Miss. Jay."

"Yes, I don't like graveyards myself. Honestly, if I can avoid going to a funeral I will find any excuse in the world not to go. I always send flowers and a card apologizing for not being there, but I just can't step foot in a graveyard."

"Many people are like you, Amanda. I better get back to cleaning the room for you though."

"Oh yes, I am so sorry for keeping you from doing your job, Edna," I reply, apologetically.

Edna heads back down the hallway to room 14, as I start getting some of my late-night work underway again. An hour passes before Edna comes back to the front desk once again.

"Hello, Amanda. I've finally got that smell out."

"Oh good. Do you know what the smell was coming from?" I ask, curiously.

"No, I didn't figure that out. I just used the industrial cleaners and the smell went away. They shouldn't have problems in that room with smells. I changed the linens and washed everything as well."

"Thank you, Edna. I know you go above and beyond. I'm sure the Johnsons will be happy as well."

"I'll do whatever it takes to get the job done right. I see you're busy, so I'll let you be for now."

"Yes, thank you, Edna. I do have work to catch up on. My lunch break is at 2:30 this morning if you'd like to join me?" I ask.

"Of course, I'd love to; I'll be there around 2:30."

"That's great, I'll see you then."

Settling back in to finish my work, I can't help thinking about what Edna said. *"Thirteen opens doors to the other side. I wonder, does that apply to all numbers equaling thirteen. Does that mean that any number thirteen? Ah, I have to quit overthinking like this...It's probably just folklore."*

As 11:30 P.M. arrives, Mr. and Mrs. Johnston come back to the front desk.

"Hi there Amanda. Does our room smell better?" Mr. Johnson asks.

"Yes it does, Mr. Johnson. Our lovely housekeeper, Edna, went extra hard to make sure that smell was gone." I respond.

"Thank you, Amanda. I love when places go that extra mile to make their guests happy," Mrs. Johnson jumps in.

"That's what we are here for. I would also like to offer you half-off your stay here tonight," I state, happily.

"That's mighty good of you, Amanda, but not necessary. Truthfully, we have been at other places that have smelled ten times worse than that room."

"I have already adjusted the billing to your credit card. Consider it our gift to you." I state, feeling satisfied.

"Well, I guess now I can't steal your towels. Ha-ha-ha," Mr. Johnson jokes.

"Well that wouldn't be amusing, Mr. Johnson, now would it? I can tell by looking at you, that you aren't like that anyway," I answer, trying not to roll my eyes.

"I'm just kidding, I wouldn't do that. Thank you for everything. I think we're going to call it a night. What time is checkout anyway?"

"Check out time is at eleven a.m. You two have a good night," I answer, smiling.

Standing there, I watch them go down the hallway, and the lights flicker as they walk by again. Shortly after, they disappear into the room.

Room 14

Walking into the room wearily, and turning the light on, we both start sniffing. All I can smell is chemicals and flowers as we walk around the room.

Brad smiles, "that smells a thousand times better. Don't you agree, Debbie?"

"Oh God, yes. That smell was bad!" I exclaim.

"I honestly figured they would put us in a different room, but we'll be on our way tomorrow…at least I hope so. The damn car just had to break down. I hope we can still make it to Calgary by tomorrow. I would hate to flake out on the house deal."

I watch the worried look on his face and try to reassure him, "Don't worry Brad. There'll be more houses if we don't." I can't help thinking, *I hope to hell we get that house. I've been dreaming about that house since it came up for sale.*

Brad smiles as he walks over to me, and wraps his arms around me as he sways back and forth, lovingly.

"I know, Debbie; I also know you wanted that house. That house has everything we've been looking for: a two car garage, a pool, and a family room to die for."

"Let's not worry about it tonight. Let's just get some sleep and hope they have our car ready tomorrow. Even if the car's not available, we can rent a car tomorrow morning if need be."

Brad kisses me on the lips passionately, then slowly pulls away and softly answers, "that's true. With any luck we'll be gone before eleven a.m. and on our way."

"I hope so. I do want that house, Brad," I answer, feeling hopeful.

After getting undressed and into bed, I listen to the sounds of the traffic going by. Looking over at Brad, I watch him getting comfortable. Staring at the ceiling, can't stop thinking about the house. Finally, I close my eyes.

A whispered voice startles me awake. Looking around, I try to figure if I am imagining it or not. I listen for a while, but nothing; a beam of light shoots across the room as a car drives by.

I close my eyes again, but less than a minute later a whispered voice calls out clearly, "Debbie. Debbie, come here. I have something I want to show you."

Opening my eyes once again, I look around but all I can see is vague lights and complete darkness. I try to wake Brad up, but he is sleeping too soundly and just grumbles in response.

Turning towards the voice, I ask, "Who are you…? What do you want?"

"Debbie. Come here… towards the bathroom, I must talk to you now," the voice replies, this time sounding familiar.

"Why?" I ask quietly, almost recognizing the voice.

"You need to know this now. Come here."

I slowly sit up and get out of bed, making my way to the bathroom. Once I am inside, the door quickly closes behind me.

"What the hell…." I shout, startled as the room lights up almost blinding me.

"Debbie. I've been waiting to get you alone."

Grabbing the door and trying to pull it open, I shout, "Who are you voice? Why have you been waiting to get me alone? Open this door right now or I will…" Fear grips me as I continue struggling with the door.

"Who I am is no importance to you right now. That door is locked, and you will listen to what I have to say."

I look around, panicked, trying to place the voice. "I can't even see you; I would believe you more if I could see you," I exclaim, looking around frantically.

"I will show myself to you soon, but I must tell you something first."

"What?" I inquire, confused.

There is a pause before the voice replies, "Walk into the shower and I will show myself to you."

Looking towards the shower, petrified, I ask again, "why, should I trust you?" I can't help but think that this is how horror movies start.

The man's voice is stern and calm as he responds, "you should trust me; I know about your husband. Walk in the shower."

Taking a slow breath, I agree, "okay. You better have something decent to tell me then."

The curse of 13

I slowly walk towards the shower, thinking to myself, *"What's going to be waiting for me inside there?"* I peer around the corner to see if anyone's in here, but there is no one. Once I step inside, however, the shower door slams shut by itself. Trying desperately to open the shower door, I shout, "Show yourself!" A light begins to form into the silhouette of a man, and suddenly I recognize him. "Grandpa? Is that you? You died ten years ago."

"Yes, my little Debbie. Did you miss me? I have missed you all these years. I have watched over you since I died, and I'm proud of the woman you've become."

"How're you here, grandpa? I... don't understand?" I exclaim, overwhelmed with emotions, tears clouding my vision.

"Easy, my precious. I'll explain soon. How've you been, Debbie?"

Moving closer to him and hugging him, I answer, "I have been good, grandpa; we are just on our way to buy a house in Calgary. I have missed you... I love you so much. You said you had something to show me?"

He holds me close to him, and his cologne smells familiar as I cuddle up closer.

"You still smell the same way I remember," I exclaim, still feeling emotional.

He rubs my shoulder and softly replies, "yes. Being dead has some perks, Debbie. How's your grandmother doing?"

"Grandma died a year ago. You didn't know about that?" I inquire, confused.

Perry Pankratz

He looks at the shower floor, sighing, "Your grandma and I were only together when you kids came by, otherwise I lived on the other side of the city. I thought your parents would've told you by now."

"No, they didn't say anything about you two being split up. Why wouldn't my parents tell me something like that?"

"I knew our son didn't have any balls. He should've said something, and your mother should've told you as well. I can't believe they would ignore your feelings like that. I am so sorry my little Debbie, grandpa will make you feel all better. Remember when you were a little girl and I bounced you on my knee? Your smile lit up the whole room."

"Yes, I remember. Grandma was always telling you to stop, but you just kept going."

"I enjoyed those times. That's what makes it so hard to tell you about Brad, though. Would you like to take a walk with me... like we did when you were little?"

"Where do you want to go?" I ask, feeling happier.

"Take my hand, Debbie. You and I are going to go for a walk where no person has gone before," he replies, holding out his hand.

"What do you mean, grandpa?"

"Take my hand, and I'll explain on the way."

I nervously grab hold of his hand and turn to face the back of the shower. Grandpa holds his hand out and continues to walk forward. The wall moves, conforming to our bodies like jelly, as we walk through it. Opening my eyes on the other side, I can feel the wind. There is sand and debris all around us.

28

"Where are we, Grandpa?" I ask, shielding my face from the blowing sand.

"We are at my home, Debbie. These wastelands of civilization… sands of time ends here. This is where people die, completing their journey."

"I thought there was a Heaven?" I ask. Everything's so ugly and broken here, and the winds howl all around us.

"Don't worry, Debbie. I used to think there was a Heaven too. I learned a long time ago that Heaven is not a place of forgiveness, and they teach us all of our lives to believe Heaven exists. The truth is that we're caught between two hells with different moralities. I found God, followed all the commandments, and this is my Heaven. Sadly, this is Hell, too. Everyone who dies comes here…"

"Grandpa, you said everyone who dies comes here. How am I here with you if I'm still alive?" I ask, confused.

"I wish you were, but you've died."

Covering my mouth, I yell, "Oh my God, you were going to tell me Brad killed me, weren't you?" Almost falling in disbelief, I think to myself, *"Why would Brad kill me? He knows I love him more than anything in the world."*

He looks at me, with an almost evil grin as he replies, "no, Debbie. I was going to tell you Brad will be joining you shortly."

"I don't understand, Grandpa? If Brad didn't kill me, how did I die?"

"That's an even longer story to tell you, Debbie. I'm not sure you want to hear it though."

Looking at his eyes, I try to make sense of what he's saying. "Please, Grandpa, tell me. I don't understand how I'm dead. An hour ago, I was breathing and just heading to bed. Tell me how?"

"You see, demons and other evils here exploit this world. Demons connect to your world. I am unsure how they do this, but once they leave through a door, we're able to pass through for a short time. That's why I came through when I realized they got you. I wanted to be able to bring you over here safely. I do not know what they do to people otherwise. I have never seen the people pass back after they pass by the arch over there."

"But how did they kill me?" I ask, trying to wrap my head around any of this.

"They do horrific doings to people. I've heard from others that they get into your head and make you do horrible things to yourself. Others say they take your soul and your body follows."

"Well, you took me here grandpa. If they do this to people, how did you manage to bring me here?" I ask, not understanding what's going on.

"Oh, Debbie. You are so smart. It's too bad you didn't realize before I snatched you here. I am not your grandpa, I am a Nightmare. I am part of the thirteen levels of the dead. I reaped your soul like a kid in a candy store. Your body, without your soul, will soon return to sand. Brad will soon be here as well. Right now, he's dreaming about some sweet demons. When you thought I was your grandpa, you yearned for the information about Brad that I had. Don't think for one moment that I care."

"Everything you told me is lies," I yell, crushed.

He looks hard at me, his eyes black as night, "oh no, Debbie, not everything I told you is a lie. Everything I said about this place is true; I only lied about your grandpa."

"Why would you do that? You're a demon? I haven't done anything to you and yet I'm here…why?" I yell, wanting to hit him.

"Oh, Debbie, because you were the easiest to get here. You see, many years ago, on the spot where your room rests, I was a young boy myself before civilization settled here. We were building a home, and one night a creature came out of the darkness of the woods. This creature, or whatever this ungodly monster was, murdered my dad and every adult around.

"Well, it's my turn," I thought, *"I'm going to die the worst possible way. Either torn apart or mauled to death."*

"After looking at me for a few minutes, the demon shapeshifted into my dad. I stood there, frightened as could be. He grabbed me and threw me up against the tree, ripping my shirt off. His word to me was thirteen. I didn't understand what he meant by that, but I do now. There are thirteen levels of the dead. The first three aren't bad, but the others are worse."

"I don't care about what happened to you! I want to go back home!" I yell, angry.

He looks at me as he smiles and states, "good, keep that spirit… you'll need it if you interrupt me again. Now, where was I? Oh, yes! When I got to level ten, I prayed to God for him to kill me. I have been searching for Heaven and Hell this whole time I've been here. I have found there are seven levels of Hell and six levels of Heaven on earth. Together, they create the thirteen levels of the dead. If I choose not to do what I'm supposed to, bring the living here, then once I hit thirteen, I will wish I were dead. Both God and the Devil will watch me in agony for eternity. That's why you're here, Debbie. I have no choice but to bring any person that stays in that room here, by whatever trick necessary. I didn't want to do it, but after reaching level ten I couldn't stand the pain anymore. I don't ask you to forgive me, and I never will. All I ask is that you understand why I did it. I am not even going to take you through that arch."

"I don't understand entirely… you mean if you don't do what God ordered, you go through thirteen levels of pain?" I ask, even more confused.

"Yes. Each time you fail to do something for the powers, your punishments are greater. I am not allowed to say what these punishments are, but rest assured you'll wish for death and death won't come," he nods a little as he speaks.

"I see so will I have to do this too?" I ask, fearful and confused.

"Only if I take you through the arch. Most of the time they don't notice if you bring them through the arch; they only notice when they are dead. You'll be fine wandering out here in the wastelands. Don't worry about food, you won't need it; the first few days you'll feel discomfort, but that's only because you spent a lifetime eating. It's just symptomatic, and once your brain realizes you are dead that will stop it."

"Why do they do this?" I ask, while thinking to myself: *"there has to be a reason behind this. Why would God do this to people? Maybe he is lying; he has lied about everything else."*

As I glare at him, he explains:

"The best I can figure is God and the Devil agreed on a deal, and that arrangement is… all living people must die. Like I say, there's no Heaven or Hell, this is both right here. Since I've been here, I have not seen one angel or one demon. I just call them all demons. None of them are good or bad, they all have the same mentality. I am sorry, Debbie, but I must go get Brad now. If I were you, I would head west. Stay near the debris of buildings and planes. Standing out in the open is just a sign for them to come get you. The last one that remained in these open wastelands became a play toy for them. On this side of the arch, you're a victim, waiting to be tortured. On the other side, you'll do as they say or be punished. I wish they would've left me on this side. I may have to run and hide, but at least I wouldn't have to take people who have much life to live yet."

"Might I ask why you are helping me? I mean, not that I'm not grateful. I'm just curious," I ask.

"I know what it feels like to become a victim before your time; I also know what happens on the other side of the arch. Truthfully, I don't want to see you in pain. I can tell you wouldn't be willing to kill innocent people like I do. You would do more good helping people on this side of the arch."

"Will you be bringing, Brad here?" I ask, hopeful he will.

He looks hard before answering, "No. Brad will go through the arch."

"Why, don't you just drop him off here?" I yell, angrily.

"I can't, Debbie. If I drop two off, back to back, out here, they will know who did it. I do not want to go through level eleven. I risked my well-being dropping you off here. In a few weeks I'll drop another one off here, but if they realize I'm dropping people off instead of taking them through the arch, it will be me who pays."

"What will become of him?" I shout, confused.

"I guess, it depends on God and the Devil. Their decision decides his fate."

"Well, thank you for helping me anyway."

"You're welcome. Remember to stay hidden. I would hate your freedom to become something worse."

"I'll remember. Thank you," I reply.

As he vanishes in the blink of an eye, I am still irritated with him for leaving me in this place, alone. I trudge through the sand to the west, sticking close to buildings and other debris along the way. My feet feel heavy as I sink in with every step in the sand. I finally come to a rubble pile that I can get into. I sit down and listen to the wind's eerie howl beating across the opening. Curling up, I wonder what is going to happen next as the reality of what just happened starts to set in. Looking out of the hole, the grey sand makes everything dull and colorless. My thoughts turn to Brad. *"Oh my God! What is going to happen to you?"*

An unexpected surprise.

Watching Brad sleep, tucked in so nice and comfortably, I walk over to him and sit down at the edge of the bed thinking, *"Oh Brad, you bad boy. That's an X-rated dream you're having. Shame on you. Cheating on your Debbie… such a dog you are. I wonder what Debbie is going to say after learning of this? Oh well, only one way to find out, right Brad?"*

I lean over and whisper in his ear, "Brad. Get up… I have something to tell you. You're going to want to hear this."

He begins to move as he opens his eyes and responds, "what's up, Debbie? Holy… 1:30 in the morning?"

Rubbing his eyes, he smiles at me. Smiling back at him, I grab his arm and rub his hand up against my nakedness while seductively whispering, "Come with me; let's go take a shower together. I'm dirty and you're the only one who can clean me up."

He looks at me and grins, "That's what I love about you, Debbie. You're spontaneous. Give me two minutes to freshen up a bit."

"I'll be waiting…" I reply, suggestively, walking towards the bathroom slow and seductively.

Feeling his eyes watching me as I saunter all the way into the bathroom, I turn back to look at him one more time. Getting to the shower, I turn the tap and water begins to spurt down. I close the glass doors to the shower and soon the steam has fogged up the glass. Soon Brad's silhouette appears through the fog, and his hand opens the door as he walks in. I grab him as his hands move over my body.

"Oh, Debbie. I love you so much!"

"I love you too, Brad! Stand up against the wall," I command.

"Anything for you, Debbie…"

"Yes… are you ready for this?" I ask, looking into his eyes as I smile while running my hand down his chest.

"Oh yes, Debbie…" Brad moans as he closes his eyes.

"Good," I whisper, leaning against him and quickly thrusting into him, pushing him through the wall. Shortly after, there's a flash of light and we fall and hit the sand.

As we hit the sand, I roll off him and he screams, disorientated, "what the hell is this place, Debbie?"

"I don't know, Brad, but I'm scared," I answer, worried.

"It's okay, I'm here, Debbie. This place seems like the dream I was having before you woke me up."

"What dream?" I ask, eyeing him.

He is taken aback at the look on my face as he explains hesitantly, "it was just a dream. I dreamed we were having a threesome with another woman. We were on a beach making out and then you woke me up."

"You were dreaming of another woman? What are you trying to say, Brad?" I raise my voice, irritated.

He gulps air as the winds blow and he tries to calm me down by holding my hand tight as he responds sincerely, "Debbie… it was just a dream; you are the only woman for me. I was just saying that the sand here reminded me of the beach."

Glaring at him, I make him let go of my hand, "sure, Brad. It seems like this whole trip was a waste. I wanted that house so much, but you only wanted another woman. Thanks, Brad. Thanks for everything. You can go to hell," I screech, loudly, trying to keep the angry tone to my voice. Brad chases after me as I stomp off, heading east.

"Debbie! Come back, please. I'm sorry... you're naked and I'm naked...we don't know what's out here. Let's stick together?"

I come to a stop and turn around to face him, "what, Brad? Do you think there's another woman out here for you to get the threesome you're looking for? Go to hell, Brad," I yell, trudging away.

"Argh... let's just try to find a way out of here, and we'll figure the rest out later. Please, Debbie... you know I would never do anything to hurt you... PLEASE!"

Seeing the tears trickling down his face, I soften, "fine, Brad. Once we find a way out of here, we're going to have a long talk about those thoughts of yours. How dare you think of another woman, especially when I was going to do something special for you."

"I'm sorry, Debbie. I don't know what I was thinking. You know I love you. I always have."

Staring at him with fury in my eyes, I yell, "I figured you did too, but I guess now the truth is out. It's better I know your true feelings."

Perry Pankratz

"A dream. How can I control a dream? Honestly, Debbie. I mean, it would be like saying I can monitor the sun and the moon and stop them at my will…well I can't! Wait. Look over there… someone's standing over there. Maybe they'll help us."

He points towards a sand dune, and I my gaze follows. "Maybe they will."

As we get closer to the human shape, I see a woman's figure standing there in a tattered dress. The expression on Brad's face suddenly drops as if he's seen her before, and she raises her hand at us.

She begins running towards us quickly, calling out, "hi! I thought I was the only one out here. Boy am I glad to see you two."

Brad looks at me, worried, and waits until she is closer to shout back, "how long have you been weathering this storm, Miss?"

She covers her eyes as the winds drift quickly by. She shouts while holding what's left of her dress close to her, "I've been here for a couple days now in this storm. I'm Michelle."

Smiling at her, I hold my hand out, "I'm Debbie, and this horndog here is my husband, Brad."

"Since you're naked I can see he's happy to see me as well. Hi, little friend."

I cross my arms as I glare at Brad. "See what you've done, Brad? We were in the shower before we fell through onto the sand, Michelle." I state, watching Brad biting his top lip.

"That's weird because I was just walking along, felt faint, and then I was in this sand. The winds have done an excellent job to my dress. You are the first people I've seen since I've been here. I am not sure where here is though."

"I don't know where here is either. We're hoping to find someone who would know," I reply.

"This place must be for nightmares, where everything goes to die. All I have seen is debris and sand. Not one person around, not even an animal."

Brad reaches out and grabs Michelle's hand as he states, "don't worry, Michelle, you can stick with us. The three of us together should be able to find something here."

I glare at Brad and he quickly lets go of Michelle's hand. "Yes, of course. You're welcome to come along, Michelle; you just have to watch, so my husband doesn't stick you," I comment, sarcastically.

"I'll make sure he doesn't," Michelle replies, stifling a giggle.

"Come on, Debbie, enough already. I apologized for that dream I had. It was just a dream… GOD DAMN IT!" Brad yells in frustration.

Michelle stops laughing and became serous. "Oh… I see what's going on here. My boyfriend had that same dream a few months ago. Next thing I know he's doing everyone but the dog."

I glare at Brad and he turns a deep shade of red. "See? I'm not the only one who thinks so," I shout.

"So, Michelle, you're saying that because your boyfriend did that to you I'm going to do that to Debbie?" He asks, furiously clenching his hands.

"My boyfriend told me that he had this dream of a threesome, and he said it was just a dream. I believed him and we continued like normal. Two weeks later I caught him in our bed, with two women! You men are the same. You say one thing and you'll do the other."

"Just because your boyfriend did that doesn't mean I would sink so low. I wouldn't do something like that. Debbie? Please, Debbie, don't listen to her, I would never cheat on you in a million years. I swear."

"Michelle, what do you think he would do?" I ask, looking over at her.

She looks at him, glancing down, before replying, "I think he would cheat on you. I bet if I bent over he'd put it right in the spot. I can see the lustfulness in his eyes."

Visibly angry, Brad yells in frustration, "oh come on already! I wouldn't. You know what... I've had enough of this, I'm leaving, you can either follow me, or you can stay here! I'm serious, I'm going."

"Okay Brad, leave. Bye!" I shout, watching as he walks away.

Michelle waves and yells, "Thanks for stopping by, Brad. It was a pleasure meeting you and your little friend there."

Brad stops and turns back at us. He screams loudly, "shut the hell up, Michelle. I'm out, Debbie."

We watch as Brad disappears over the horizon of a sand dune.

"So, Nightmare, do you think he realizes where he's headed?" Michelle asks, breaking the silence.

"No. I can't wait to see the look on his face when he gets there, though," I reply.

"That will be priceless one to see."

"Yes, especially when he sees who he runs into."

"Jesus Christ, you're bad, you know that?"

"I know. If I weren't, I wouldn't be Nightmare," I proclaim, smiling at Michelle.

Break time.

Looking at my watch, I see that it's almost time for my break and walk over to Julie.

"Hi! If you have everything under control here I'm going to take my break now," I explain.

Julie looks and smiles as she replies, "oh yes, of course. I'll be fine until you get back."

"Great, I'll see you in a while," I answer.

As I walk down the hall the lights flicker and go out. I open the door to the staff room and see Edna sitting at a table. Grabbing a cup of coffee, I sit down with her, "Hi Edna. I wasn't sure if you were going to be here yet or not."

"Hi Amanda, I just got here a few minutes ago," Edna replies, glancing at her watch.

"After we finished talking before I was looking through the logbooks of luggage left behind. Have you noticed room 14 has the most luggage left behind?" I ask, curious. I can't help but think of her story, *"perhaps Edna is right about a 'curse' being on that room."*

"I've never thought about that," Edna replies, shaking her head.

"I found that rather weird myself. Do people just get in such a hurry in that room that they leave their luggage behind and never return?" I inquire, shaking my head.

"I know there have been a few times where the people are trying to rush around and forget something, but it's usually not a whole suitcase."

"I know I have never left that much luggage behind. That reminds me: as long as the people don't complain about the smell, I won't worry about telling Josh about it if I don't have to. That was an awful bad smell."

"Oh yes, that was. I'm glad I could get rid of it. I keep thinking about what we were talking about earlier, Amanda. I was thinking, could there have been unholy people on this ground? Perhaps an Indian burial ground that was disturbed?"

"I am not sure, Edna; can I ask why you're wondering?" I ask, intrigued.

Edna looks around and leans closer as she mutters, "I was just thinking about the possibility of something happening like what happened to my mom when she was a kid. Perhaps someone's buried under the building, and the building is stepping on the grave."

"Well, that would explain the strangeness of room 14. How would a person go about getting rid of something like that?" I inquire.

"We would need to know the person buried there, and then we would need to make a blood sacrifice."

"Oh yes, I forgot about that. I'm just worried… there's so much luggage left behind from that room. What makes it worse is that this started at least six years ago from what I can tell," I state.

Edna looks puzzled as she replies, "six years ago? I only started four months ago, but that could mean someone may have introduced something into that room. After those people check out I'll bring in a friend who deals with malicious entities. She might know what's going on."

"I started two months ago, but nothing like this has happened before. Earlier I just got this spine-chilling feeling and wanted to get the heck out of the room."

"Yes, I remember I scared you. I'm still sorry about that."

"Don't worry about it, Edna. I've just never felt like that before, in that room or any room," I exclaim.

"Sometimes when there are unknown spirits around that's when you'll get those feelings. I am sure there is something in there. It might spook some people, and that's why they leave their luggage behind. Tomorrow evening I'll bring my friend with me to work and we can check it out then."

"That sounds good, Edna. Maybe we'll get some answers," I reply, feeling a little better.

"I hope we get to the bottom of this. I would hate to think anyone is being scared, or worse, getting injured."

"I'm sure there's nothing much, just something spooking the people." I reply, trying desperately to believe my own words.

The curse of 13

The door swings open and both Edna and I turn our heads as George walks in, shouting, "Hi Edna. Miss Jay. Must be lunchtime."

"George, did you ever figure out what was wrong with the lights?" I ask.

George shakes his head as he heads to the coffee maker and explains, "No, Miss. Jay. I think we'd have to get right into the walls to discover the problem. I wouldn't worry about it, though. They are only flickering every so often. When it gets a little slower we'll take the wall apart."

"Okay, George, I'll put it on a list for after the busy period. It's already 3 a.m. though, so I'll talk to you both later. Enjoy your lunch," I exclaim, hurrying up to get back to work.

"Talk to you later, Amanda."

"Talk to you later, George." I respond, waving to both of them.

Walking out of the staff room, I head for the front desk. As I walk, I look down the hall where room 14 waits. I continue to the reception and relieve Julie. I check over to make sure there hasn't been a complaint from room 14, and to my relief there is nothing, I head to the office and continue my days' work, stopping after a few moments and reaching towards the shelf to grab the ledger.

I can't stop thinking about room 14, *"why so many bags left behind? Where are these people going? Perhaps the video cameras have caught these people leaving in a hurry?"*

Grabbing a request form from the desk, I fill it out with the dates and times from the ledger documenting the abandoned luggage. Finally signing my name, I place the form in the outgoing mail.

I know you.

I've been walking for what seems like an eternity in these sand dunes. The winds are so blinding I can barely see, but still I call out, "Debbie? Are you there, honey? I'm sorry. You have every reason to be upset with me."

As darkness looms overhead, strange sounds come from the distance, almost like a hoard of zombies coming my way. I try to go the opposite way of the noise, but I can hear them getting closer; I start running in the sand but trip over something hard. Looking back, I see glowing eyes coming towards me. I crawl over to a piece of debris and try to make myself invisible. A short time later, the glowing eyes and vague outlines of people begin to appear around me.

"Get up you coward," a voice screams at me

Another voice shouts, "do as you're told; get up before you feel the edge of my sword."

"Okay, don't hurt me, I'm getting up," I yell, getting off my belly and onto my knees before finally standing up. I can see silhouettes clearer now, "who are you and what do you want with me?" I ask, frightened.

"How dare you ask us questions? You are on our territory; you have no rights to ask anything," the first voice bellows, slapping me in the face.

The second voice shouts, "Get to your knees and beg for forgiveness you piece of crap. How dare you insult the Lord? Be glad I don't bring my sword across your neck."

A third silhouette emerges, and I gasp in recognition. "I know you...you're Jesus," I whisper, surprised. *"Am I dead? How is this possible?"*

He stops in front of me, kneeling, and softly replies, "yes."

"Oh, thank god..." I shout happily.

His face turns angry as he shouts, "don't mention my father's name again. He's the reason I am out here in the wastelands."

"I'm sorry. Please forgive me," I reply, confused.

"I'll forgive you this time. Don't ever mention his name again, or Gabriel will bring the sword across your neck and divide you into two. What brings you to our territory?"

"My wife and I were taking a shower and then suddenly we were here. I don't even know where I am!" I exclaim.

Jesus looks around, his eyes shifting all over before stopping at me again.

"Where's your wife then?" He replies.

"We're separated now. I had an argument with her and walked off," I respond, tears filling my eyes.

"You left your wife alone in this place? There are monsters here that'll rip people apart. You don't even know where you are, but you leave your wife alone to fend for herself?"

"How was I to know? I didn't mean to leave her alone, I just walked off to cool off and then she was gone."

Jesus glares at me, his stare cold and unforgiving, as he states, "Stupid. I'll tell you where you are. You're in the wastelands better known as Heaven. That arch there, there's Hell."

"I thought Heaven is supposed to be a beautiful place? The Bible says that Heaven is everything you want it to be. Jesus, why is it dark and gloomy? I don't understand why it looks so...?" I respond, confused.

"So disgusting? My father and Lucifer have a partnership; after all, they're best friends. They decided that instead of fighting sins and evil, they would turn Heaven and Hell into this. This place represents both Heaven and Hell, but I've been on both sides and neither is worthy of the name Heaven. We are but scavengers trying to make our way here. My own father left me here to rot. I remember the day as though it was yesterday. We were sitting at the table, around the time of America's Civil War, having breakfast when the Devil, or Lucifer if you prefer, came walking in. I went to strike Lucifer down when my father took my power away and told me to sit down. Of course, being a good son, I sat down, and the Devil sat down across from me. I listened to them talk as if they were old friends; they discussed a great many details of what they were arguing about. Human beings were the root of their arguments and hatred. As I sat there, listening to them, I felt sickened by what I was hearing. My father said there was no hope for humankind and he wanted to make them pay."

"What? Why does he not have faith in humankind?" I ask, watching, as he moved closer to my face.

"He thinks you are worthless and pathetic. I would say you are lucky to be here with me! Where was I? That's right. The Devil talked a lot about purgatory and my father agreed in saying that nobody should ever live. So, my dad and the Devil sent their armies to purgatory. I watched firsthand as the Army of Light and the Army of Darkness invaded the sanctity of purgatory. I watched as angels and demons worked together to slaughter the men, women, and children who were within this once sacred place. Within 50 years, purgatory became this barren wasteland of destruction. I prayed for them all, but father caught me praying and I was once again put on the cross to suffer. My own father struck the nails into my hands while Lucifer hit the nails into my feet. How is a son supposed to feel when his own father and his nemesis worked together? I watched from on top of the cross as my dad turned this beautiful place of Heaven into a dark pit of Hell. Then not much later, the Devil created the tsunami that filled Hell with water thus bringing Hell to an end. These last couple of years have strengthened their bonds, and now they are working together to destroy every human of life. Given enough time, they will succeed."

"You're kidding… right? There is no way they can win," I reply.

"I wish I were. We see your kind coming here all the time, and lately there's been an increase in the amount people. Gabriel was kind enough to take me off the cross. Gabriel and Daniel are the only ones who still believe the same as I. So, now we wander in these wastelands trying to survive, against my father and the Devil. Every day we're seeing more people handed over to them, and if they find our hiding places they'll raid us. You know that lump you feel in your throat when something's wrong? That is the impression that we have every day here. If your wife is here, she'll be their little buttercup by tomorrow. That's why I called you stupid. A woman here doesn't last long, and if she's on her own it'll be even shorter than that. Men don't even last that long whether it be because we have to kill them for nourishment or because they're trying to kill us."

"May I ask how come you haven't kill me then?" I ask, cautiously.

"You were cowering. Most men try to prove they're men by attacking us. We'll never strike down a man when he's down. That's what saved your life. I'm sorry to say your wife is no more. Father and the Devil sit at the same table in this wretched place. You can join us or you can walk alone."

"Can I join you?" I ask, hoping to avoid being killed.

"You can, brother, but remember if you try to attack anyone of us you'll die. You must do everything we say, that is your only hope for surviving right now," he replies, patting me on the shoulder.

"I swear I will, Jesus. I will do whatever you ask," I reply, smiling.

"Good. We need more meat like you to help us fight on. Now get back up, let's go before they spot us."

"I'm sorry, Jesus, I think I may have misheard you in the wind here… did you say you needed more meat like me?" I ask, a confusion of thoughts swirling in my head.

"I did. You see, you will feed us in our time of need. You at some point will sacrifice yourself when the enemy comes. Seeing you haven't been here as long as we have, there's a good chance that you will be the next one to die, and we will pray for you. I call all new people meat, but if you survive I will call you by your given name. On the other hand, if you don't survive, I won't have to feel sorrow over your name."

"I understand," I reply, while looking at them all.

We walk as the winds howl, and Jesus wraps his face with a scarf as we head towards some buildings. Sheltered, we listen to the winds blow, ominous sounds coming from all around. As we walk, I can't help but ask questions.

"What creatures are out here?"

"There are a large number of beasts out there: flying creatures, ferocious animals, ones that will snatch you up from underneath your feet. The worst ones are the ones that try to infiltrate our ranks by saying they're lost."

"Wait? Do you mean me, Jesus? Are you trying to say I'm one of them?" I shout, fearfully.

"Yes, that's what exactly what I mean. You see, every day we run across people like you. People who try to keep us out in the open so my father and his 'friend' can find us. That's why you're going to the cross. My father and his friend can have their sniveling little snitch back. You thought you could fool me? The jokes on you."

"What are you talking about, Jesus? I have done nothing wrong. I'm not a snitch and have been truthful," I shout, confused.

"Sure, that's why we watched you walk here with that beastly boy Nightmare. Did you think you were going to pull it off? You don't think we know that's a shapeshifter? That man does bidding with and for my father and the Devil on the other side of Heaven's arch. You're no better than my father... traitor. Hang him!" Jesus shouts.

"What are you trying to say? That's my wife, Debbie. We were going to have fun in the shower, and then we fell through to here. I didn't deceive anyone; you saw me with my wife and then that woman Michelle showed up. Is that who you're talking about?" I ask.

"I know who I'm talking about. We saw you walking together with that shapeshifter. He is a vile evil and you'll hang on that cross. Whether you think that's your wife or not does not matter. No, we have too many people's lives at stake to believe you."

"Please, Jesus, don't. How can I make you believe that I am not one of them?" I plead, a lump building in my throat.

"You can't! You see, we used to find people, but since my father and the Devil became good friends I can't trust anyone anymore. I'm sorry. They have sent many people to find us, and they have used many different tactics. I want to believe you, but I just can't trust anyone anymore except for the ones who have been with me from the beginning."

"I understand you want to test my faith, so be it. I will show you I am on your side even if it costs me every last drop of my blood. I will show you," I reply.

"Good for you, my son. May this bring peace to your thoughts? If you have any sins, I will forgive you for them right now."

"I have no sins. I have always been faithful to my wife, and my word has always spoken true even when I wanted to deceive."

"Then son, you are a saint. One day we'll honor you as a saint, but for right now you'll have no honor. May peace be with you?"

"Jesus please, I beg of you, don't do this…" I shout, watching Daniel and Gabriel walking towards me.

They grab me as I fight back until Gabriel pulls a knife. Looking at the knife in my face, I stop fighting and they drag me over to a wall where two beams meet to make a cross. They forcefully hold my hands against the cross beam as Jesus approaches, a hammer and spike in his hand. My screams go unheeded as I feel the point of the spike press hard against my hand. A loud bang and the spike goes deep into the wood, through my hand. The pain is unimaginable, but there is no one around to hear my screams. I try kicking my legs, but it is no use and they hold me down. Jesus takes out a longer spike, presses it against the top of my left foot, and slams it through both feet in one hit. They all stand there watching me scream in agony.

"I would suggest you don't scream too loud. The monsters are everywhere and they can hear well, even through this wind. I know it hurts, I've been through it. The pain will subside," Jesus says matter-of-factly as he turns away.

I watch as Jesus walks away, but Gabriel remains, smiling as he holds his sword close.

"I guess you wish you had said that word one more time and received my sword across your neck, huh? Soon you'll be with your friends, once again plotting against Jesus. I'm glad this is you, and not me."

I gasp for air through the agonizing pain trying desperately to say something. I muster enough air to say one word, and I scream: "God!" They stop abruptly. Gabriel looks back and walks towards me. The look on his face tells me he isn't going to help me.

He smiles as he shouts, "A little too late, but if you want to feel my sword, I'll indulge you."

Gabriel pulls out his sword, raises it in my face, and turns it from one side to the other. He stands there as if he's deciding whether he should or not, until he swiftly thrusts it through my abdomen. I let out a scream as the pain is unbearable. The last thing I see is him walking away, laughing, before everything goes dark.

Not another one?

"Good morning, Miss Jay. How was your first night as manager?" I ask.

"Tiring after working days. Especially the shift the day before, Mr. Harding. I think we did well, though; we only had one check-in last night. Room 14. There was a complaint made about the cleaning staff yesterday morning. They left an awful smell in that room; I compensated half of their bill, because of it. They're not mad as Edna was able to clean the smell while they were out," Amanda replies.

"Okay. When the morning staff gets in we'll have a meeting and see who was responsible for leaving room 14 a stinking mess. I'm glad to hear you were on top of these problems, Miss Jay. Now I know I put someone good in charge of overnight," I reply, impressed.

"Thank you, Mr. Harding. I did enjoy working overnight; getting all the paperwork done is easier when the interruptions aren't as many. There was one item I added; I put those lights in the hall because they keep flickering. I had maintenance come up and check them out. They figured it'd be okay until we hit the slow period and they can take apart the wall to see inside."

"Okay, I've been wondering myself if I should or not. I'm glad to see you were on top of it. I'll let you get going so you can go get some sleep; you look tired."

"I am, Mr. Harding; I'll try to play catch-up while I can. You have a good day, Mr. Harding."

"Thank you, Miss Jay. I'll see you at six," I reply, smiling as I look her over once more.

"Goodnight, Mr. Harding or, rather, good morning. My bad."

"No worries, Miss Jay, I did that too when I changed from days to nights. I'll see you at six." I exclaim, watching as she walks out the door.

I head to my office and close the door to get some work done. Just after eleven, there's a knock on my door. "Come in," I call, sternly.

Angelica opens the door and states, "excuse me, Mr. Harding, but I've tried to call room 14 about their check out time and there's no answer in the room."

"Again with room 14?" I answer, annoyed, as I look at the ledger. "Mr. and Mrs. Johnson. Thank you, Angelica; I'll deal with it from here."

I pick up the receiver and dial.

"Okay, ringing. Come on, pick up the phone. Time to go check them out," I mutter as the phone rings unendingly.

Standing up, I head out of my office, grabbing the passkey along the way. As I walk down the hall, the lights begin to flicker as I make my way to room 14. I knock on the door a few times and call out, "excuse me, Mr. and Mrs. Johnson? Check out time is eleven a.m..."

I can hear water running as I turn around and head back to my office. Stopping at the front desk, I leave instructions.

"Hi Angelica, it sounds like Mr. and Mrs. Johnson are taking a shower. Let me know in an hour if there is still no answer," I state, frustrated.

"Yes, Mr. Harding, I will."

Heading back to my office, I close the door and start writing out a new policy changing the checkout time to noon before I continue with my paperwork. As I continue to work, another knock on the door interrupts me.

Angelica opens the door and states, "housekeeping is cleaning room 14, and it looks like Mr. and Mrs. Johnson left in a hurry. They left their bags and the water running."

"What? Again?" I reply, annoyed. "We are going to have to stop putting people in that room. That's the second set that have left their luggage behind. Did they return the key card?"

"They left the key cards on the night tables."

"Well, at least they were decent enough to do that. The last guy took his keycard with him. I'll write out tags for the luggage and you can get the maintenance men to take them to the storage room with the others," I state.

"Okay, I'll tell housekeeping to bring the bags to the front desk and then I'll call maintenance," Angelica responds, nodding.

Closing the door behind her, I reach up and pull the ledger down, scanning the page for room 14's entries. I think to myself, *"that's crazy... no one leaves their entire luggage behind."*

The phone interrupts my thoughts and I answer it. "Hello? Yes, we have a few rooms available. For today? Okay, what time? In an hour? Yes, we'll have those rooms available and cleaned by then, Mr. Penny. Okay, thank you. Bye."

Getting up, I head to the front desk. "Hi, Angelica?"

"Yes, Mr. Harding?"

"Do we have any reservations?" I ask.

"I don't see any here, Mr. Harding," she replies, clicking through the computer.

"Okay, good. We'll have all the rooms booked tonight. In an hour Mr. Penny will be in to sign for every room in the hotel. Could you tell housekeeping, please? We'll have to change the sign to no vacancies and unavailable. Sounds like this one is going to be a loud one. It's a vacation with the whole family by the sounds of it," I state, happy for the business.

"My goodness. So, we're talking grandparent's parents and kids?"

"The whole works."

"Okay, I'll get housekeeping to go through all the rooms to make sure they're clean. I'll switch the sign to no vacancy as well."

"Thank you, Angelica; I don't know what I would do if you weren't here," I reply.

"You would probably do it yourself, Mr. Harding. Ha-ha."

"Yes, you're probably right, but I'm glad you're here to help me."

I watch as the staff hustle to get everything ready as we wait what is sure to be a nightmare of epic proportions. Shortly before three, cars begin pulling up into the lot. Children and parents come walking in, and the kids run down the halls. Finally, an older man walks up to the desk, and I watch him as he talks with Angelica for a few moments. She looks my way, as he walks over to where I am.

"Hi, I'm Mr. Henry Penny," the man says, extending his hand towards me.

"I'm Mr. Josh Harding, a pleasure to meet you, sir," I exclaim.

"Likewise. I am glad you allowed us to stay here. You would be surprised at how many places expect complete quietness. Don't get me wrong, we intend to keep the children in check, but one cannot keep children quiet one hundred percent of the time."

"Oh yes, we understand that most children have energy to get rid of," I respond.

"Thank you again, and if anything is broken or damaged, please charge it to my card and let me know right away. I hope they don't, but just in case."

"Yes, of course, Mr. Penny. Enjoy your stay."

I was told west was the way to go.

I keep camping in the debris, moving further west slowly. I can only hope I find something soon. I see something walking by, and he looks angry. I hope this wind cloaks where I am.

"Oh crap. I don't think, I'm going west anymore. That building should've been behind me, not in front. Damn sand," I think to myself.

I get up and turn around and start heading the way I just came. After trudging through the sand for an hour, I hear voices in the distance. I try to find a place to hide, but there is none. I am a sitting duck out in the open. I can hear the voices coming closer and panic begins to set in. I drop to the ground in hopes that they do not see me. I can hear the multiple voices coming closer to me, and I wonder what they will do to me if they catch me. I listen as one of the voices appears to have noticed me.

"Look, there's someone over there," a man shouts.

"I can't see. Oh! I can see them now. Who're you?" His companion shouts at me.

"I bet that's Jesus's damn crew. They're always creeping out here."

"How many can you see? I see four people. No, make that five."

"What should we do?"

I look around in confusion. "What? They can't be talking about me. Where are the ones they're talking about?" I whisper. All I can see is sand and buildings.

"Let's go the opposite way of them; we'll die without proper equipment to take them on right now."

I hear them coming towards me, and think to myself, *"Don't see me... oh my God, here they come. Please don't see me!"*

One of the men trips over me, and the rest stop. I make a pained sound from the impact, and the man speaks.

"Well, who do we have here?"

"Please, don't hurt me. I'm just trying to hide," I plead, putting my hands up.

"Well, you're not doing a good job of it. A lady! In this open space? You sure as hell don't want to be here when Jesus and his group get here. Unless of course you want to die?"

"I don't want to die. I just realized I was going the wrong way, so I turned to come back and then I heard your voices," I say hastily, afraid.

"In here there's no right way. You're only possibility of surviving is hoping for the best. I'm gathering you're new to this place?"

"Yes. I was lured here by someone called Nightmare, and he told me to go west."

"West? There is just barren land west of here. Perhaps he was thinking the opposite way of Jesus. You're welcome to join us, but I can't promise you'll be safe. At least you won't be alone."

"Thank you. I guess groups of people are better than wandering aimlessly alone in these wastelands. What was that about Jesus? Isn't he a good guy? My name's Debbie by the way," I say, extending my hand.

"Glad to meet you, Debbie. My name is Ray. Let me give you a hand up? The Jesus you learned about is far different here, and I would not want to meet him either."

"Really? So, are you part of Heaven or Hell?" I ask, curiously.

"Well, before Heaven and Hell came here, this used to be Purgatory. Let's get moving. We'll talk as we walk; it'll be safer that way. Purgatory was where everyone would come before moving on to Heaven or Hell. A long time ago, Lucifer and God came together and they decided Purgatory was unnecessary. They sent angels and demons to destroy this place. They turned this once beautiful waiting room into what you see before you. For some reason, they came after us and killed everyone in Purgatory. They didn't leave a man, woman, or child alive. Since then, people unknowingly come into these wastelands. If you are lucky enough, you get to stay on this side. The other place isn't so great. You stand a greater chance of living here… over there you must do whatever God or the Devil wants you to do."

"What? Are you saying God and the Devil killed everyone here…together?"

"Yes, that is a big reason there is no happiness in the afterlife. You're either damned, or you're damned. At least being with us you stand a little more chance of living to see another day. There are some you'll have to watch out for, like Jesus. Nightmare is another one, but I find it odd that he told you to come this way. He works for them and does their bidding. I do have a sneaky suspicion God and the Devil want to take care of humankind for good."

"That's what Nightmare said, too. I just don't understand why they would do that?"

"There are only two people that have that answer, and I don't think we're going to get the answer from either one of them. We fought our best for Purgatory, but it was just no match for what they had."

"I'm David, by the way," the third man intervened. "They rushed in like a stampede. We got our fair share as well, but as Ray said, in the end they beat us. Now we've got Jesus on this side, I don't know if he's worse than both of them put together. Whatever you do, don't fall for anything he says. You'll hang on the broadside of a cross. I know I've heard stories of what happened between him and his father and Lucifer. Some say he was wronged when God and the Devil got together because they no longer wanted him to be part of the expert plan."

"Why would God do that to his own son though?" I ask, confused.

"I don't know. As David said though, these are just whispers in the air we've heard. More gossip than anything else. We could rack our brain's day in day out thinking about it, but you'll still come up with the same answer. Most times we just try to stay away from them if possible. That's no joke. If you see him, run the other way, even if there is a monster waiting for you."

"Seriously? Is he that bad of a guy, David?" I inquire, a little frightened by what they're saying.

"Oh yes, he is. I think so because he figures he got the short straw. Ray may say differently because he's on this side of that arch. I mean, Jesus went from being right under God as his son to losing his power and his livelihood. God and Lucifer go way back, and now they're back together again. So now he and his clan continue to kill anyone on this side, probably to gain control."

"You're right, David. If he controls this side, he can stop them from getting to the arches. I like your way of thinking," Ray chimes in, nodding.

"So, what are you trying to say? Once he kills everyone here he'll get back in his father's good graces?" I answer, confused.

"That's exactly what he's saying, Debbie. If Jesus were to run this whole side, he'd be in control of the arches. You see Debbie, no matter where in the world these doors are, no one goes straight to Hell or Heaven. I don't think he would hold it for long, though. His father and the Devil would stop that quickly," Ray explains.

"You got that right, Ray," David says. "There's no way in hell they would stand for that. They might even crucify him again."

"How do you plan to stop him?" I ask, looking at them curiously.

The curse of 13

"We just keep running. You can't go up against something unless you have something to go up against him with. Right now, we have no weapons that will go toe-to-toe with him. You see what they've done to Purgatory. They took everything we had away. We barely fled with our lives. I wish we did have something to use against him, but I feel that it's going to be a long while before we can hit him."

"How long have you been running? I mean just running?" I question, watching their faces sadden.

"Since shortly after they attacked Purgatory and destroyed it. You have to understand; when they came they came with a vengeance. They slaughtered everyone in sight. There wasn't a man, woman, or child left, and they didn't care."

"That's so heartbreaking. I mean, it makes no sense to me. I know, I'm new here and have no idea what I'm saying, but it just seems senseless to kill everyone."

Ray looks at me, tears in his eyes, as he answers, "Yes, it was senseless. The best guess David and I can come up with is that they wanted every living person dead."

"Have people tried reasoning with God or the Devil? Surely God still has to have some goodness to him?" I ask, trying to find some answers for a peace.

"Whatever goodness he did have, is long gone by now. We have thought about renegade angels and demons forming alliances, but then God and the Devil would have closed up shop already. There is no stairway to Heaven and there's no highway to Hell. That's why they needed Purgatory. Purgatory gives them the best place to take the living from. They don't have to wait anymore. Before, when people died, they came to Purgatory. It was like the waiting room of the dead. It would give people a chance to realize they were dead before moving on. With Purgatory destroyed, they get more shock value. People don't have time to take in that they've died before they go to Hell," Ray states.

"I see. Have people escaped from this place?" I ask, hoping to get back home.

David looks towards Ray, and then me before answering, "do you mean, back to the living?"

"Yes. I'm just curious."

"Unquestionably not. You see, once you pass through to this side, your body returns to sand. That's the one sad part. With thirteen in place on this side, thirteen on your side becomes a doorway to this side."

"What do you mean thirteen? Oh… you must mean the six levels of Heaven and the seven levels of Hell?" I ask, trying to understand what they are talking about.

They both look at me weird and David replies, "I'm surprised you know that. But yes, anything thirteen is acceptable to their doors; it doesn't even have to be the number thirteen. Say you have cards stacked thirteen high, they can open the door there. Objects that equal thirteen can become a door. Something where you were staying must have equaled thirteen to bring you here."

"We were staying in room 14. There's no way it could've been that," I insist.

"The clock maybe? Something in your room had to have equaled thirteen."

"Nothing I can think of," I answer, trying to remember if there was anything at all.

"Didn't that last guy say something about room 14 as well?"

"Yes, I think you're right, Ray. I'm sure he said he was staying in number 14," David replies.

"Do you know where he was staying? We were staying at Happy Hotels," I say, looking between them.

"It does sound familiar. Was that where he was staying, or maybe it was another person. Something links that room to these wastelands, Debbie."

"I don't know. I was sleeping and I was awoken by a voice calling my name. I got up, headed to the sound in the bathroom, and when I was in there he slammed the door closed. He told me to come to the shower, and I did, and that's where I saw my grandpa. He said he had to tell me something, and that he wanted to go for a walk. He crossed me over and then showed himself. He told me to head west before disappearing," I exclaim.

"Sounds like something in the bathroom had something to do with thirteen..."

David jumps in excitedly, "no, Ray! She said she was sleeping when she heard the voice... You know, the more I think about it, it was probably the room itself. The only way to contact the living like that would've been to have that person in the realm."

"I'm sorry what are you two talking about? Realm?" I repeat.

"Okay, Debbie, I'll try to explain this to you as best I can. You see, you're in the wastelands now, but you were in the living world."

Ray shouts as the winds continue to howl,

"I get what David means," Ray interrupts. "From the look on your face, I see you get it too. I can't believe we didn't get that connection before. The room must be the thirteenth place. I bet the living world is full of superstitions."

"That makes sense. I know my friends used to throw salt over her shoulder for good luck. Some people wouldn't cross a black cat's path. I know several places remove thirteen from their buildings unless they're with other numbers. How do we get this message out to others?" I ask, with a new hope.

"We can't, we just have to hope they figure it out on their side before people come, learning too late what'll happen," Ray says.

"We could if we could produce enough power to talk to the other side. The only problem is the two that hold power aren't going to let us use it," David interrupts.

"That's true. The only one that's able to get that little bit we need is Debbie," Ray counters.

"I don't know what you two are thinking, but I'm not going into that hellhole!" I exclaim, thinking to myself, *"I'm not killing myself for these guys."*

"I wasn't thinking of that. For some reason, Nightmare likes you much more than most. After all, Nightmare didn't send you towards Jesus, he sent you west."

"He told me though; he's already on his tenth level. He said they get thirteen chances before he'll become riddled with pain forever," I answer, hoping to find a way to get back at him.

"Tenth level sounds like he doesn't like the rules much. Could be a loaded gun if he would help, but then we would need to find him."

"He never said anything to me about seeing him again. He just told me to run west and keep going," I reply.

"Shoot, that won't work then. One day we will finally figure out a way to stop them."

"Sorry. I wish there is more I could do to help."

"Don't worry, Debbie. We'll keep doing what we do best... running until we figure out a way to beat them," David replies.

As we continue to trudge through the sand, the wind howling, we hear a scream in the distance. We come to a stop and all look towards where the sound came from.

"Sounds like Jesus got someone," David says, lowering his head.

"What do you mean, David?" I ask, confused by what he is saying.

"He means Jesus just crucified someone. That's the only time I have ever heard a scream that loud," Ray explains.

"Oh my God. Brad. He's out there. Nightmare said he was going to be here soon," I exclaim, screaming inside.

"I'm sorry to hear that. If that was him, he now belongs to Jesus," Ray says, matter-of-factly.

"No. We have to find him. Please. We have to..." I plead, as tears stream down my face.

Ray puts his hand on my hand and explains, "...I'm sorry, Debbie. That's why Jesus does that. He's hoping we will come to try to help so that he can kill us all. I'm sorry, but he is lost."

Cry for the children

Kids screaming up and down the halls were not what I was expecting to find today coming on shift. I think to myself, *"Now I know why Mr. Harding wanted me to come in early... ass!"*

Finally, a friendly face walks towards the desk and I exclaim, "Hi, Edna! We won't be able to check the room out tonight."

Edna looks at four kids running down one hall and replies, "I heard it's a packed place this evening. That doesn't matter anyway; my friend couldn't come this night. She had a prior engagement she couldn't get out of. She did tell me a few interesting things. She made reference to thirteen."

"Thirteen? What's this thirteen again? I know it was last night we talked about it," I ask, trying to remember through a cloud of tiredness.

"She said that thirteen is a doorway to the other side and that on particular days, thirteen can open a time and place. I think she was kidding, but I can't say for sure. She was in a rush, and then she mentioned the dead. Sherry was running around washing linen, so she might not have heard what I asked her. She didn't stop for two seconds while I was talking so that's probably why I didn't understand what she was saying."

"That's possible, Edna. I know when I'm in a rush I tend not to listen to what another person is saying. I did look at the ledger again, and Mr. and Mrs. Johnson left their bags behind as well." I reply.

Edna looks puzzled as she replies, "they didn't seem hurried. They left their bags like all the rest did? That room has evil in it, I'm sure of it. There's something in there making people disappear. I mean, I would never leave my bag anywhere, and I've even rushed around like a chicken with my head cut off. There have been hundreds of bags left behind and most from that room. I'd say something fishy is going on in there."

"I would have to agree with you, Edna. Do you know which of these people are going to be in the room? I don't; they've been coming and going since I got here. Later tonight I'll check and see if adults are in the apartment," I reply, worriedly.

"Okay, I'll try to keep an eye out as well. You look tired, Amanda."

"I am, Edna. I got home this morning and my neighbors were loud. I think it was about 2 p.m. before I got to sleep. I had to be up by four to be here for six and got called in early. I think I'll be as useful as a dead horse tonight," I exclaim, wanting to collapse from exhaustion.

"Don't worry about it, Amanda. You'll get your stride. No matter how tired you are you'll be on top of the game again. Believe me, I've done it myself."

"Thanks, Edna, I can always use a boost. I have a coffee break coming up at eight if you'd like to join me?" I ask.

"I think I can arrange my coffee break around then. Okay, Amanda, you take care for now and I'll see you around eight," Edna says, walking away from the desk.

"You as well. I'll see you at eight."

Back behind the desk, my thoughts return to room 14. *"What is in there that makes people disappear? Something that makes people vanish, but leaves their luggage behind? I remember the old saying: you cannot take it with you when you die. They returned their passkeys but left their luggage in the room. And why would there be sand in the shower? Were they trying to clog the drain? I'm going to have to check the housekeeping logs and see what they say. Mr. and Mrs. Johnson did not seem like the type to just leave either. I wonder what's in that room. Oh well, I had better get back to work. Come on, I have to get my mind to focus. Focus, focus."*

"You alright, Amanda?" Vanessa asks, bringing me out of my thoughts.

"Huh? Oh yes, sorry mind is elsewhere right now, Vanessa." I reply, smiling.

"Oh okay, just making sure."

"Not a problem, thank you. If you need anything, I'll be in the office." I state, as I walk into the office and close the door.

As I sit down, I look over and see the housekeeping book. I reach over to grab it. As I flip through the pages looking for room 14, I see that it's been cleaned. I close the book up and put it back on the ledge. As I continue with my paperwork, I want to look in the book again, but wait until it's closer to eight. I finish everything, and then grab the book again. Looking through it, I'm astonished by what I am seeing, and lose track of time.

"Oh shoot, it's about eight!" I say to myself, getting up and heading to the staff room after letting Vanessa know I'm taking my break. Edna is already waiting there when I arrive.

"Hi, Amanda, I hope you don't mind, but I got you a coffee."

"Hi, Edna. No that's fine I can use one," I answer with a smile.

"So how is your day going so far, Amanda?"

"It's going. I'm tired, but I'll make it through. I did find some interesting answers about cleaning room 14 though," I state, trying to focus.

"Oh? What did you learn?"

"Did you know that every time room 14 is looked over, there is always a bunch of sand in the shower? Only in room 14 though," I state. I can't help but question how no one has noticed this before.

Edna sits back in her chair with a concerned look on her face. She sits there for a moment deep in thought before replying.

"Every time? I knew there was sand in there the last time I cleaned out the shower. Well, no what I would consider sand. It had a more grayish tint to it like grit."

"Grayish? There's nothing written about the colour, just sand. I wonder why?" I reply.

"We usually don't mark the specifics; we just put sand or dirt."

"That's true, Edna. There's never been a real need to mark details unless there's damage. Tonight, ask some of the other housekeepers that have cleaned room 14 what they may be seen."

Edna still looks concerned as she replies, "yes, I can ask them about it. I'm sure the rest will tell me if there was anything like that. On a side note, those kids are brats. They're running all around the second floor and even knocked over one cart. Do you know how long they're staying?"

"I could hear them running up and down the stairs, too. I think they're staying for two or three days. I'd have to check the check-in sheet to know for sure. Let's hope they calm down by ten o'clock," I state.

"Yes, but that's still two hours to go yet. I'll need to drink my lunch tonight to get through this day."

"Truthfully, I think these kids are going to keep me awake tonight regardless of the noise. It's going to be interesting for me. Edna, I thought you don't drink? You said you had a drink on your birthday, and that was it," I answer.

"I know, but I could use a drink still. These kids are going to drive me nuts," Edna smirks.

"Just stay out of the limelight. They can't annoy you if they can't see you," I reply, laughing.

"I'll hide in a broom closet. No, I've got some work I can do in the basement; I'll hide down there for a few hours."

"You're evil, Edna. I'll probably stay in my office," I state, laughing.

"You'll be in your office, and I'll be in the basement. I think I can put up with kids for an hour and a half."

"Oh yes, I better get back to work myself, though. I'll talk to you after, Edna."

"Yes, I should get back as well."

Getting up and throwing my garbage away, I wave to Edna and head back to my office. I look down the hall and see kids running all over the place, and a man, walking towards me.

"Excuse me, Miss?"

"Yes? How can I help you today?" I respond.

"Yes, I was wondering if it was possible to use the main floor for the kids."

"Yes, that would be fine. Please just let me know what room they will be in. They would have to be quiet by ten as the other guests may complain," I explain, hoping they are quiet much earlier than that.

"Oh yes, they would be silent. I just wanted to make sure it was okay to leave the kids on the main floor here."

"Yes, that's no problem. Anything else I can help you with sir?" I inquire.

"No, that's all I needed. Thank you for your time."

"You're welcome. If you need anything else, I'll be in my office doing paperwork."

"Thank you, that's good to know."

I walk back to my office and stop at the front desk. Looking through the papers, I try to find out how long they're going to be here. "Three days? Shit!" I whisper.

"What's that Miss Jay?" Vanessa replies.

"Oh, sorry Vanessa, I was just looking at the sheet," I explain.

"Oh, you saw that too," Vanessa smiles, leaning in closer.

"I'm guessing that's going to be a long few days and nights," I reply.

"Yes. I'm glad I don't have to work 24 hours here, I'd go nuts from the noise alone," Vanessa smirks.

"I hear you loud and clear, Vanessa. I'll be in my office if you need anything; I have to catch up on paperwork," I reply, feeling exhausted.

"I imagine. A little peace and quiet wouldn't hurt either."

"No, it doesn't. If you need anything, you know where I'll be." I respond.

I head to my office and close the door behind me taking a big sigh of relief. *"I hope these kids go to bed soon. It'll be a race to see who goes nuts first, them or me,"* I think to myself as I sit down and start doing the paperwork.

Ten o'clock rolls around and I head out to make sure all the kids are out of the hallways and staircases. When I'm satisfied there are no more running around, I head back to the office, giving Vanessa a smile on my way. A half-hour later, I come out of the office and walk over to Vanessa.

"Which parents are in 14, please?" I ask.

"Let me check… Ed, Tammy, and Vern. It says on a note they will be arriving tomorrow."

"Okay thank you, Vanessa," I respond.

I walk back to my office and close the door, taking a seat. Looking through the housekeeping book again, I try to find something noted about room 14, but there's nothing but sand and dirt written. I close the book and start placing everything in order for when Mr. Harding arrives.

I need help.

It's one-thirty in the morning, and I'm back in room 14. Coming out of the shower and making my way towards the bathroom door, I stop. Looking around the room, I think to myself, *"four children, and all girls, too! I have been waiting for you four for so long now; I thought it would never happen. Now, what do children like? Let's see, girls like dolls."*

Floating around the room checking everything out, I see some dolls lying around. After a few minutes of searching, I'm face to face with a coloring book. I flip through the pages, finally stopping. I make my way to the bathroom again and call out in the darkness, "Denise, Emma, Amy, Carol!" awakening the ones in the room from their slumber. They slowly begin to get restless and finally, one by one, they sit up.

"What? Who's there? How do you know my name?" Denise calls out.

"Mine too. I can hear you," Emma adds.

"Why can't I see you?" Carol asks.

"I'm scared," Amy whispers in the dark.

I watch as they look around worried, and I answer reassuring, "don't be afraid, girls. I'm a friend, and I'm looking for new friends. Would you like to be friends? I would like you all to be my friends."

"I can't even see you?" Denise whispers, looking around with fear in her eyes.

She gets out of bed and looks as If she's going to run out of the room. "Give me one moment, Denise, I'm coming. Can you see the light?" I say, before she has the chance to escape.

I slowly walk out of the bathroom until they can see me.

"Yes, I can see the light, it's getting brighter," Denise answers.

"I can see you too. What's your name?" Emma asks.

I grin as I walk closer and respond, "my name's Peter..." Their faces expose smiles and the fear seems to dissipate.

"I know you! I've read about you before," Carol shouts, excited.

I nod as I make my way to the edge of their bed, "that's right. Would you like to come to my place for some fun?" I inquire, watching their faces closely.

"It won't be fun, but you all are going to help me get what I want. After all these years, finally I have found the gold mine. Now, I better make sure nothing goes wrong. I better make it sound convincing," I think to myself.

Emma raises her hand and asks, "Where's the other one? The one with the fairy dust?"

I'm puzzled as I try to remember that little thing with wings... "Ahhh. Oh, I don't need fairies. You see, I've got something much better. Would you like to see it?" I ask, smiling, pulling out four rocks from my pocket that make the shape of a heart.

"We would!" The girls reply in unison.

"Each of these shiny rocks allows you to come with me, and unlike that little fairy you mentioned, you can keep them forever," I state, holding them out in front of me. I watch as they stare at them with awe in their eyes, as they twinkle and glow.

Emma looks at me with an innocent smile, her brown hair mussed up from her sleep. "We can?" She asks, getting closer to my hands.

"Yes. What colors would each of you children like?"

The other three also come closer, and I feel warm inside looking at their glowing smiles.

Emma points excitedly to the red glowing piece, "I want the red one!"

Her hand reaches towards mine as I pass her the first one. "There you go, Emma. A bright red one for you," I reply, smiling.

Denise's eyes glitter in the darkness as she comes closer and looks at the stones, her black hair in a ponytail. She points and asks, "Can I have the yellow one?"

I pass her the stone as Amy creeps closer. Her dark blonde hair is mussed up, and there is an innocent twinkle in her eyes. She points to the orange one, "can I have the shiny orange one please?" She grins as I hand it to her.

"That leaves bright pink for Carol. Now, will you come with me on an adventure?"

Emma gets out of the bed and walks up to me, holding the stone in her hand, gently. "Can you tell us a story first, Peter?" She asks.

"All right. What story would you like to hear?" I ask.

"A story?" I think to myself. *"Shit! Let's see. I'll tell the story of these assholes and what they did to everyone!"*

"I know, tell us about an adventure you were on!" Carol suggests.

"Okay. I'm a little rusty on my storytelling, so bear with me a bit. A few months ago, I came across this mean man with an army behind him. This man's name was Ged. He is a vile, evil man that fools people into believing the monster is on their side, but he's not. If you trust him, he'll hang you and torment you to no end. I came across him when I was on my way home, and my friend was with me. He told us about great deeds he had done. He said he battled evil every day and wanted us to join him. I didn't trust a word he said. I could tell he wasn't telling the truth, and I tried to tell my friend that, too. My friend wouldn't listen, though, and now they have him guarded by evil people. These people shoot fire and throw electrical bolts, so I can't get my friend back. That's where I hope you four can help me," I state.

"They're that bad?" Denise asks.

I nod, continuing, "You are all innocent. Their evil fire and electrical bolts is no match for you four. They will run and hide from you; you might even be able to defeat them. Once you defeat them, you can all take on Ged himself with a little hatchet I have. Sadly, my friend doesn't have long because the monsters there get hungry. I don't want my friends to die; do you four think you can help me?" I ask, pleading.

There is silence for a moment as they all look puzzled until Denise pipes up. "I'll help, but that's not much of a story, Peter."

"I'm not good with stories, I'm better with adventures."

"What'll we battle these monsters with? We don't have any weapons," Amy asks.

"Oh, but you do, Amy! You see, your heart can break the evil spell and shatter the monsters if you believe. Do you trust me, Amy?"

"I do! I believe!" Emma jumps in.

All four stones begin to shine brighter and brighter, and the girls look at them, amazed.

"You see? The brighter the stones get, the more you believe, the more you think, and the faster you can defeat them. Are you all ready to go?" I ask.

Denise leans in to the others and whispers something to them before turning to me. "I don't know about the rest of you, but I am going."

Emma nods as she looks at Denise and shouts, "I am too! Let's go defeat the bad people and bring happiness back to his home."

Amy looks at me, unsure, but turns to Emma and agrees. "Yes, I do, too. I can't wait to see their faces when we come."

"I want to see that Ged destroyed. We'll be the champions and they'll even throw a parade for us," Carol says in a soft but excited voice.

"Everyone will throw a parade for you four. Once we defeat them, everyone will come out of hiding and they can rebuild a New World again. Everyone will hug you when we're through with them. Come this way, young ladies, we'll go through the magic door," I reply, as we head to the bathroom and into the shower. I look at their faces as I begin to explain. "Okay... this is how are going to go through," I say, putting my hand on the back wall. "Everyone ready?"

"Yes... Let's get them!" Emma shouts.

Emma goes first, and the rest of the girls follow. Lastly, I cross through the wall. We appear in the wastelands, and they all look around, disheartened.

"What happened here, Peter?" Denise asks quietly. "Everything's destroyed and there's nothing but sand and broken buildings," she says, tears welling in her eyes.

"Ged did this; he came through here and destroyed everyone's homes. People ran in fear and hid everywhere to get away from his wrath. That's why it is important we defeat him...so people will come back again. Once people rebuild this pleasant land, everyone can be happy again. Are you ready to help me?"

Denise's eyes water as she looks at the destruction and decay. She sighs and looks at the sand, then into my eyes. "Yes, I will help you. We will help you."

"That's great. Let's make our way to those arches over there. Once we're there, we'll be in their den. Once we're in, we can slaughter the heartless monsters that hold my friend," I state, holding back on what I really want to say.

"Heartless my ass. Those soul-sucking bastards. Today I will be free of their tyrannical ways. I will make them pay, and it's all thanks to these girls," I think.

"That's a long way away, shouldn't we fly or something?" Emma asks, tugging on my robe.

I look down at her, smiling, and reply, "no. If they see us coming, then they'll be ready for us and even capture us. We don't want that."

"That's going to take us too long to get there," Denise argues.

"No, Denise. You see, we travel faster by foot than by flying. These are evil winds that are blowing here to slow people and make sure we don't kill Ged," I explain.

"So, this sand can blind you, Peter?" Amy asks.

"Yes, Amy. The gravel gets in your eyes only when you're flying and then you can't see people. They weren't stupid when they designed this place. So long as we're on the ground, we're safe from anything they throw at us."

As we continue to walk towards the arches, and the winds blow hard, I listen to the sounds of voices coming from all around. An hour of walking later, and the arches of Hell become more visible. "Just a little bit further, girls. We're almost there. We'll kill all the monsters."

"I hope so, there's something that's behind us," Carol replies, worried.

"Don't worry. As long as we're moving in this direction, he'll not harm us. He's there to make sure that nobody attacks us," I state, looking back.

"Is he going to protect us, Peter?" Emma asks.

"He is the Walker; he's making sure we get to the arches unharmed," I reply.

Looking around the wasteland, I'm trying to spy one particular man. *"Come on out, Jesus. I can smell your rottenness in the air. I know you're close. Are you going to track us and try to stop us at the arches? Yeah, that's what you are going to do, isn't it?"*

"Walker? That's a silly name for someone," Amy says, interrupting my thoughts.

"It might be silly, but he's had that name forever. You see, he makes sure people get safely across dark places."

"Oh okay. Hi, Walker," Amy says, turning around.

After another half hour of walking, the gates are a mere fifty yards away.

"Well. Well. Well. What do we have here? My old friend, Nightmare!" A voice calls out to us.

"His name is Peter!" Emma shouts back.

Jesus looks at her with anger as he continues, "what do we have here, Nightmare? Another one of your games to feed my father and his best friend?"

"Oh, poor Jesus. So prophetic of you. You used to be the apple of your daddy's eye, but now you are little more than a murderer. Sitting out here, in the wastelands, hoping one day you will be able to kiss your father's feet so nicely again. What a shame you just couldn't be more," I reply, shaking my head.

"Still better than you, Nightmare," Jesus says, glaring at me with his hate filled eyes. "At least I'm not doing their bidding for them. I mean, how old are these ones? Between five and ten? At least I still hold the honor I used to."

"What's he talking about, Peter? Why does he keep calling you Nightmare?" Denise asks in a small voice.

"I'll explain later, don't pay him any attention. You hold no honor, Jesus. Since you can't enter here, you have done nothing to help these people. All you do is kill and maim people. You have nothing, and you'll never have anything," I reply, smirking.

"I got a message for you to send to my father. Tell him either he dissolves that friendship of his or he's going to pay. I know how he works his little plan here; I'll make his life worthless to the human side."

"Oh please, Jesus. You've been around for 2000 years and haven't done squat to help anyone, but yourself and your father. You two are nearly in the same barrel. You get people flocking to you in masses, and if they don't agree with you, well then time to go. At least I still have the heart to care. What did you do with poor Mr. Brad?" I exclaim, watching as he looks at the children.

"You know what I did with him. You don't think we were watching you the whole time? We are aware you sent him to try to kill us. He learned his lesson and Brad's suffering is the results of his decision."

"Oh please, he had no idea who I was. He thought I was his wife; I harassed the crap out of him to make him leave. You always fall for that one, that's why you'll never be more than what you are, Jesus. What's going to be even funnier, for me anyway, is when I tell them that you stole him from me. How are you going to explain that to him?"

"How dare you place that on me? You know you did that on purpose. When he finds out the truth, your hurt will be far greater than mine. I should take these girls with me."

I stand in front of them, glaring at Jesus with a coldness of death, "you even touch one of these girls and you'll be dead before you hit the ground. Face it, you'll fail again. Why don't you just go back and crawl under the rock you came from?" I exclaim, watching his every move.

"I'll make sure my father knows the truth," Jesus mutters back, glaring angrily.

"You can't pass through the barrier. What are you going to do, scream from out here? You know your dad has nothing but distaste for you after that stunt you pulled. I mean, you thought you were going to kill them both? That was a laugh and a half for me. Even I could've come up with something smarter. Taking on both Heaven and Hell, with 2 billion angels and demons, and only one you? All because you couldn't stand having the Devil sit by you," I goad, laughing at him.

"Peter, why are you talking about Heaven and Hell?" Carol interrupts, obviously worried.

"Don't worry, Carol, I'll explain after this loser leaves," I state, watching him closely.

"I'm not going anywhere, Nightmare. We have unfinished business and we're going to deal with it right now."

"No, Jesus, because unlike you, I have a job to do. Let's go, girls. We have to kill Ged," I reply, turning to go.

"Who the hell is 'Ged'? Someone they created to come here and kill me?" Jesus screams after us.

"Don't worry, Jesus. You'll find out soon enough. Besides, I know you like surprises, so I will leave it at that," I state, a smile forming on my face.

"Damn you, Nightmare. I will kill you for this."

"As always, you are welcome to try, but you'll still die. Bye Jesus, have fun in your paradise," I answer, as we continue on our way.

Oh no, not in there!

Hearing a woman scream down the hall, I jump out of my chair. *"What the hell's going on out there?"*

"Excuse me, Miss? Have you seen four girls running around the hall here?" A woman shouts, hysterically.

"No, I haven't. Why what's wrong?" Vanessa asks, trying to calm the woman.

"Our four daughters are missing!"

"What're their names? From which room? Which floor?"

"From room 14. They were there at ten when we left them, and I just went to check on them a few minutes ago and there's no one in the room! I'm Karen Fern, and my daughters Denise, Carol, Amy, and Emma are gone!"

"What? No one was supposed to be in that room until tomorrow. Okay, just let me get the manager, I'll be right back."

I can hear their conversation, but there's a knock on the door before I can get there.

"Come in," I answer, knowing it has something to do with the children and room 14.

"Sorry for bothering you, but I have a woman, Karen Fern, out here who says her children are missing from number 14."

The curse of 13

"Missing from 14? I didn't think anyone was supposed to be in there? I reply, concerned.

"Room 14 was supposed to be vacant until tomorrow. She said she checked on them at ten and midnight and it was fine, but now, at just about one-thirty, they're gone."

"Did you see any children running around in the hall?" I ask, hoping it wasn't the curse of that room.

"No one's been through the lobby since about eleven."

"Okay, check the security cameras for me, please," I ask, as we walk out of my office.

I head to the front desk where a panicked woman stands.

"I'm Miss Jay, the night manager. Can you run through this with me, Karen? What happened?" I inquire, seeing the concerned look on her face.

"We put four of our children in the room, Denise, Emma Carol and Amy. They were there when I checked at ten and again at midnight. I figured I'd go check on them before heading to bed, and now they're gone. Just gone!"

"Okay, and what's your name again?" I inquire.

"Karen Fern and my children are Denise, Emma, Amy, and Carol," the woman states, visibly upset.

"Karen Fern? Weren't you checking in tomorrow?" I ask, confused.

"Yes, we were, but we caught an early flight and got here eight hours earlier than expected."

"Who checked you in?" I ask, still a little puzzled.

"Mr. Harding!"

"Okay… I see he has you written as Mr. and Mrs. Vern, not Fern. Vanessa is going to check the video feeds and see if your children came out of the room. I'm going to go look in the room and I'll let you know what I find, okay," I explain, trying to stay calm.

"Yes, whatever you have to do, but please get my children back," Karen responds, pacing in the lobby.

"Okay, Mrs. Fern please have a seat. We will do everything in our power to find your kids," I reply, motioning for her to sit down.

I run from the front desk into room 14, and when I get in there the rotten smell from yesterday is back. Looking at the beds, from the way the covers are pulled back it seems like they got out of bed. I go into the bathroom and look around, but I don't see anything. I can't stop thinking about that awful smell, and it feels as if ants are crawling all over me.

A loud bang brings me out of my thoughts again.

I turn around and notice a bag fell over. I continue over to the shower and open the door. On the bottom of the shower is a pile of grayish colored sand. I slowly step into the shower, avoiding the sand, and place my hand on the wall, the next wall, and then the back wall. As my hand makes contact, I feel a slight tug and my arm starts going through the wall.

"Help me!" I scream, as my arm disappears into the wall, pulling the rest of me along.

I grab onto the shower door, and it slams shut on my hand, making me let go. When I open my eyes, there is sand hitting my face. I stand up in the sand and look around at my unfamiliar surroundings. The wind howls and sand blows all around me. "Where the hell am I?" I scream, hoping to get an answer back.

I look around and see buildings and debris in disarray, searching for something to explain where I am. As I walk, it feels as if I'm trudging through mud, and I can barely make out anything two-feet in front of me.

"Denise…Amy…Carol…Emma!" I yell as I walk.

"Amanda?" I hear a familiar voice call out.

I stop, looking around and trying to see anything, "Mrs. Johnson? Where are you? I can't see you," I answer, my heart pounding out of my chest.

"I'm coming towards you, stay where you are!"

I continue looking around until I see three people, with a fourth silouhette no too far behind them.

"Hi, Amanda. Boy am I glad to see a familiar face here."

"Where the hell am I?" I ask, confused. She is accompanied by three men, two in white robes and one dressed in tattered clothing.

"Well, according to these men, this is purgatory. Or it used to be. If I'm to believe what I've overheard, welcome to Hell," she explains.

"Hell? Holy cow. This is what happened to the people who stayed in room 14?" I ask, trying to piece everything together.

"Yes. We should get moving though, Jesus Christ was chasing us a while ago," one of the robed men answers me.

"Jesus Christ? Why would he be chasing people? He's our lord?"

"Don't worry; he's not the guy we learned about in school. It seems he likes killing people. You see those arches over there? That is where God and the Devil conduct their business. Let me introduce you to my friends here, this is Ray, David, and Frank. This is Amanda, she works at the hotel. Sorry, I should say worked at the hotel. You're dead now after all."

"Dead? I just came through the shower. I don't even understand how," I reply.

"As did I, and I am now dead. Obviously, God and the Devil are out to kill all of humanity."

"Oh my God. The grayish color sand in the shower is the same color as this sand. That makes sense now. We were trying to figure out why people were disappearing without their luggage. The back wall of the hotel's shower in room 14's bathroom must be a portal to these wastelands," I suggest, putting another piece in place.

"Yes, I was brought here by someone called Nightmare. He posed as my grandfather that died ten years ago. I followed him into this place and I've been running ever since. That's when I met these three, and I hope no one else comes through into here."

"I hate to break the news to you, but four young girls have come through here recently. That's why I'm here actually. I saw the grayish sand in the shower, and I was hoping to find those kids and bring them back," I respond, angrily.

"You don't think Nightmare took those kids do you, Ray?" Mrs. Johnson turns to ask one of the men.

"If they were in that room, then yes, I believe he did," Ray replies, a distraught look on his face.

"What's this Nightmare, or whoever you're talking about, Ray?" I ask, listening close.

"He works for God and the Devil, bringing them people who have died. You see, God and the Devil don't want purgatory because while in limbo, it means they have to wait. They figured they'd cut out the middleman and go straight to the heart. After that arch, there's another version of Heaven and Hell."

"Oh my God, that's terrible. Is there anything we can do to save these children? I don't want children to be hurt because I couldn't figure this out earlier," I exclaim.

"No, unfortunately there's nothing we can do, personally. The most we can do is hope they have a quick death."

I glare at him coldly, "you've got to be kidding me. They are only children. God wouldn't be that mean, would he?" I ask, in disbelief.

Ray looks at the arches in the distance, squinting, "yes, he would be that mean. This isn't the God you learned about in school or life, this is the God that exists today. The Devil and God made a pact, and it's been hell on earth since. It's been hell here, too."

"Oh, those poor children. We can't stand by and just let this happen to them," I exclaim, feeling saddened.

"Do you know how many children there were, Amanda?" Ray asks.

"There are four of them," I say.

David looks at me, his eyes showing sorrow, "well, I'm sure they are going to make them suffer unless Nightmare dropped them off in the wastelands. They'd be suffering here too, Amanda."

"This Nightmare sounds like a monster, David. Who would lead children to this godforsaken place and leave them to fend for themselves?" I ask, maddened by everything.

"Well Amanda, he is a monster, but he wasn't always a monster. I didn't want to have to say anything to anyone, but he used to be a normal human being. You see, after purgatory's destruction he managed to escape into the wastelands; I'm not even sure how he died. I heard he was taken through the arches, and now he's known as Nightmare."

"We best keep moving, Amanda," Ray says, tapping me on the shoulder and looking around nervously. "It's dangerous here, out in the open in the wastelands of purgatory."

We trudge through the sand and I can't help but think to myself, *"those poor kids lost in this place. Oh God, how awful. I have to do something to help them, but what?"*

Panic

Hearing a loud scream coming down the hall, I quickly turn to look. Fear grips me as I run towards room 14, finding Karen standing outside the room. Her hands cover her face as she points inside the door.

"Vanessa! There's been some screaming coming from inside the room," she tells me, tears in her eyes.

"Was it Amanda?" I ask, worried.

"Yes," she nods her head. "She went into the bathroom and a short time later she started screaming."

"You stay here, I'll be right back." I answer, touching her arm as I walk into the room, heading for the bathroom. A weird feeling comes over me, and I feel that I should get out of the room. As I walk into the bathroom, there's an empty, musty smelling sensation.

"Amanda? Are you here?" I whisper, as I peer around waiting for something to jump out at me.

I walk over to the shower, open the door, and look inside to find a pile of gray sand sitting on the bottom of the shower. Reaching down, I grab a handful of sand, and I feel a pull coming from the back of the shower. I drop the sand, and as I do the feeling goes away. I walk out of the room I stop in front of Karen.

"Are you sure Amanda went in there? She isn't in there," I ask, growing concerned.

"She did go in there. I saw her myself. Even that guy there saw her go into the room," Karen whispers, nodding.

"Excuse me, sir? Did you see a woman going into the room here?" I ask, worried he is going to agree.

"Yes, she was wearing a uniform like yours."

"Okay thank you, sir. There is nobody in that room, so I think we better call the police," I state, my mind working on overdrive trying to figure out what is going on.

"I already called the cops. They said they would be here in a few minutes," the man replies.

"Okay, I am going to close the door and lock it. Nobody else is to go into this room," I demand.

A million thoughts are racing through my head. *"What the hell am I going to do? First four kids and now Amanda. Shit is going to fly... oh my God..."*

"Don't worry; I won't go in there. Not after that scream she let out," Karen answers, interrupting my thoughts.

I walk back to the front desk and pick up the phone to call maintenance up to reception. As I'm Standing there waiting, a small group of people begin to gather around room 14. The police and James finally show up, almost simultaneously.

"Someone called about missing children?" The officer asks.

"Yes, that woman right there, Karen. There's also a missing manager," I state, pointing her out to them.

"A missing manager, too? Nobody said anything about a manager," the officer says, looking confused.

"Yes, the manager went into a room 14. That's where the four children that went missing were," I try to explain.

"Okay, so you're saying the children and the manager all disappeared from room 14?"

"Yes, they were all in 14 when they disappeared. I've looked over the video feed, and no kids came out of that room. I have seen the footage where they went in, but nobody comes out of that room except Karen," I explain, trying to cooperate with them in every way.

"May I see this video? It sounds like you're saying they should still be in the room."

"That's what I'm saying, yes. They should've been in there still, but they're not. I found some gray sand in the shower, but other than that the room is empty. I'll pull up the footage if you want to come around and take a look for yourself," I say, pulling up the security footage as he walks around the corner.

"You can see where the parents bring the children into the room, but if we fast-forward, no kids come out of there. Later, Amanda goes in and doesn't come out either. Lastly, you see where I go in and come out shortly after, closing the door," I narrate as I click through the video.

"We are going to check the room out; may I have a key?"

I give him the key card for the room, "this is the key to get into the room, officer. Please, find Amanda and those four young girls," I express.

"Thank you."

I watch them walk into room 14 and disappear. About a minute later, I make my way from the front desk just as I hear gunshots come from the room. Everyone hits the ground, screaming in panic, including me

"BANG! BANG!"

A moment later, a police officer comes out of the room, his gun pointing behind him. He looks pale as he addresses the crowd.

"Okay people, there is nothing to worry about. One of the officer's firearms accidentally fired. Please leave this area."

Standing up slowly, I walk over to that officer. "What happened?" I ask, looking at the fear on his face.

"I think we know what happened to those children and your manager."

"What happened?" I ask inquisitively.

"Well, we made our way into the bathroom, and as one of the officers checked out the shower, something grabbed him and pulled him through the wall. Another officer went to help him and went through the wall, too. I don't know exactly what you have going on here, but I would suggest you don't use this room again. We shot at the wall but the bullets disappeared. The strangest part is that as they were going through the wall they were turning to gray sand. I don't understand what's going on, but that room is a crime scene now. Don't say anything to anyone about what I've told you, okay?"

"I won't say anything," I reply, looking at the crowd still lingering.

"Good, now make sure nobody comes down this hallway until we give the go-ahead."

"Do you want me to remove the people from their rooms?" I inquire.

"I think the gunfire did that for you. I saw a few people hitting the ground on that floor."

"Okay, I am going to go back to the desk if that's alright?" I ask, wanting to get away from the guns.

"Yes, that's fine. Just make sure no one else comes down here," he nods, his gun still pointed into the room.

I walk back to the desk, hurriedly, looking back to room 14. As I walk into the lobby area, people stare and chatter amongst each other. As I look back down the hall, the lights flicker almost constantly. The officers are clearly shaken up, and one of them has his hands covering his face. Just looking at it, it must have been bad in there.

An elderly woman walks up to the desk, interrupting my thoughts, "excuse me, Miss?"

"Oh, yes. Hi ma'am, how may I help you?" I answer, trying to smile.

"Yes, I am just wondering what's happening down there?"

"Oh, I'm sorry. There was a little mishap and they should only be there for a little while longer," I respond, trying not to say anything.

"Okay, thank you," she responds, looking skeptically at me.

"Have a nice evening ma'am," I answer, smiling at her as she saunters by, staring down the hall.

I go back to watching the officers as they pace back and forth, and soon more officers walk through the front doors.

"This is going to turn into a circus, and I am right in the middle of it!" I think to myself. *"Shoot, I wish Amanda were here. She would know how to deal with this mess."*

Hanging around

"Sounds like Nightmare's up to it again. It's likely that more than one came through this time."

I look around, trying to see what Ray means. "I didn't hear anything," I say, trying to listen for anything other than the wind.

"Did you hear how that wind picked up twice, Amanda? When the winds pick up, that means someone passed through the barrier. I'm sure Jesus will get them, or Nightmare will."

"Shouldn't we go back and help them?" I ask, concerned.

"That wouldn't be the wisest of ideas," Ray replies, shaking his head. "We've been in the open for too long. The last we want is for them to know we are out here."

"You came back for me; shouldn't we return the favor?" I state, angrily.

"Amanda, we came back for you because you were right there. They are now where you were when we found you. The time it would take us to get back there… they'll either be with Jesus or Nightmare, and they'll be there waiting for us. We can't afford another loss."

"Come on Amanda," Debbie intervenes, "these men know more than we do. The weird creatures and the winds I've seen here are enough to freak anyone out. I think we'd be better get out of here."

"Yes. I know that must be hard to swallow, four young girls in the wastelands, but sometimes for the greater good you have to sacrifice one or two people. I haven't heard any screams yet, so they're either coming this way, or they've already died."

"Fine, I'll follow you, but I hope to hell nothing happens to them," I reply, looking back towards the direction I came from.

"That's fine, Amanda. You can be mad about it all you want, but isn't your life worth a little bit more than sacrificing yourself for unknown dangers?" Ray responds.

"I know what it felt like when I came through. I didn't know where I was, and I was glad to see your friendly face," I reply, trying to get them to realize what coming here feels like.

"Yes, I know," David replies this time. "It is possible they are finding their way, but the other possibility is that Nightmare pulled them through which would mean they're headed to the arches. That also explains the lack of noise coming from them. Believe me, I have been in your spot before. I want to save everyone I can, but there comes the point where you have to say, 'what about me?' You would've made a great person in Purgatory, but here and now you have to take the time to think about yourself. I also realize if anything happens to us, Jesus will be there to pick up the slack, and then everyone's screwed."

"I do get what you're saying, David. Okay, let's just get out of this wind," I concede, saddened by the situation.

We continue to walk until we find the debris of a room. It is tight, but there is an opportunity for the five of us to hide inside. We head into the broken-down space, out of the wind and sand, and sit for a while. We hear two voices in the distance, coming from outside, and make ourselves even smaller in the area, trying to remain unseen. Five minutes go by before I see two silhouettes come into sight.

"HELP! Hello?" A voice hollers. "Where are we? Can anyone help us? We're lost and can't find our way back to where we came from... Anybody?"

Listening to their voices call out, I can't help but shout back, "In here, don't hurt us!"

"Where?" The voice calls back. "I can't see anything but sand. Don't worry, we're not carrying any weapons."

My companions try to keep me quiet, but I start banging on a piece of metal until the unknown figures come our way. Once they get closer, I realize they are police officers. They crawl inside the already cramped space.

"What're you doing here?" I ask, relieved they are okay.

"We were called to Happy Hotels," the officer with dark hair explains. "Four children and a manager disappeared. We went into the shower and I grabbed some of this grayish color sand and next thing I know I was thrown into here. Randy here came in right after me. What the hell is this place?"

Looking at them, their faces are full of doubt and fear.

"I am the manager you're looking for, but I haven't found the children yet. As for where we are, welcome to the better side of Hell," I answer, thinking,

"The better side of Hell? We aren't dead though... are we Keith?" Randy pipes up, looking scared.

"I think what Amanda is trying to say is this is Hell," Ray takes over for me. "This used to be Purgatory and, to make a long story short, God and the Devil run that side of the arches, and Jesus is trying to kill everyone on this side. I can't make it any clearer or shorter than that."

Keith looks at Ray, puzzled, as he asks, "I don't think I want to ask. How do we get back to where we came from?"

"I'm sorry to tell you this, but you know that grayish colored sand that you picked up? That's the remains of your body and probably mine too. You are dead," I try to explain, still not entirely understanding it myself.

"What do you mean dead? I don't feel dead," Randy asks.

"Don't worry, it will sink in soon enough," Debbie pipes in.

"So, where we headed?" Randy asks, changing the subject.

"Right now, we're on the run from Jesus. Turns out they're not like the Bible says they are."

"That's crazy. How'd they get it wrong in the bible?"

"Go stand out there; find out how different he is from the book," David interrupts. "You see, officers, the Jesus living here is from the other side of those arches. He wants humanity and his father to pay and killing every single person is his plan to achieve that. So yes, we are running from him."

"That's unbelievable," Randy replies, shaking his head. "I still can't believe we passed through the wall like that?"

"That's a hard reality to believe, but once you accept that at least you have a fighting chance here," I answer.

We sit there, and the wind picks up again for a second.

Ray looks out the opening of our shelter and speaks, "sounds like another one just came through."

"Another what just came through what?" Randy asks, puzzled.

"Another person died. You men made the same wind sound when you came through," Ray explains.

"Well, we've got to go back and save them," Keith says, looking at us all as if we're crazy.

Ray shakes his head as he looks them both in the eyes and states, "no, that's why we didn't come for you. There are two horrible people out there. One is Nightmare; he'll take you through to the other side of those arches. The other is Jesus, and he'll kill you if he catches you. So, officers, we are going to stay right here, as we did while you two came to us."

"You can't be serious. You knew we were out there and you were just going to let us die? What kind of people do that?" Randy shouts clearly irritated.

"The person that does that is the person that lives to see another day. The rules here don't apply the same as they do for the living. As I said, there are only two choices here. We don't have the weapons to go up against Jesus, and Nightmare is on a mission. That mission is to wipe out the living. Staying out of their way right now is our best choice until we can find something to use against them."

"Are these people serious?" Randy addresses his partner. "I don't know about you, but I'm going back to help whoever came through. Let's go help whoever is out there, Keith. Let them hide like children afraid of the dark."

"I'm with you, Randy. Let's go help them," Keith replies, glaring at the rest of us.

We watch them as they crawl back out into the sandstorm and head back the way they came. Soon their silhouettes disappear into the unknown.

"Are we just going to let them go?" Debbie asks.

"Yes, Debbie. They won't make it. Jesus is probably already there. On the other hand, Nightmare might already have them. We don't take these decisions lightly, and please don't think we do. We are doing what's best to survive for now," Ray replies.

"I know, but there's got to be something we can do?" Debbie asks, hopefully.

Ray looks at me, and then the others as he answers, "there is. We can hope they come back, quickly, because if Jesus catches them we'll all be dead once they speak."

Looking at Ray, I speak, "they wouldn't tell Jesus where we are. They're police officers; they have an oath to uphold."

Ray looks at me. His eyes say he cares, but the rest of him doesn't. "Yes, Amanda, they probably do have an oath to uphold in the living. But here, their promise means nothing. Their pain is what will make them speak. You must remember. If we know people come through when the winds blow harder, Jesus knows the same, and he can move a lot quicker."

"Well, then I hope they come back," I answer.

"Even if they come back, we won't be here when they do. We're going to have to get moving again. We can't afford to be in this small space. Come on, let's get going."

We crawl out of the space and start walking again. We get half a mile before we hear a scream in the distance.

"Looks like Jesus got himself another victim," David says, turning in the direction of the sound. "Let's move quickly before we're sensed by Jesus or any of the ones following him."

Balance of time

We come up to a man who is just standing up, looking panicked as he sees us.

"Who are you, and what am I doing here?" He shouts out.

"I am Jesus. The question should be who are *you*?" I state.

The man looks fearful as he replies, "my name's Frank Ortiz. I don't know how I got here. I was looking for children who went missing in a shower and then I..."

"Well Frank, I hope you don't mind if I'm 'frank' with you? You see, we have tons of people come through here and all of them have been Nightmare's friends. I would like you to make me believe you are not his friend," I say, looking at him pitifully.

"Nightmare? I have no idea who he is. I work for the police department in forensics. I was just collecting some samples of the gray sand and next thing I know I'm here."

"Frank, I want to believe you. Trust me, I do, but I am just having a hard time feeling the sincerity in your voice. Let me tell you a little story about this place. You know who I am, but why am I here. My father became best friends with Lucifer. I live here now and this is my home. I have to be careful about the people I let in here. What do we have here, Frank? Two more people?" I shout, angrily.

"Hello?" A man's voice calls out. "We're here to help you. Just let us know where you are."

"Come closer. I see you have your friends with you. I knew you weren't telling the truth, Frank. How dare you backstab your Lord?" I shriek, shaking my head.

"I didn't backstab you, Jesus. They must been the two officers that came through the shower before me."

"Who are you two?" I ask, sternly.

"I'm Randy and this is Keith. Frank, what are you doing here?"

"I was taking some samples out of the shower…"

"SHUT UP! Now, you three listen to me. As I was saying before I was so rudely interrupted, this is my home. Nightmare has been a pain in my side for a long time, so I've been trying to find bait. He always sends people to try to kill me and he has tried every trick in the book. Now, since I figure you three are friends of his, I think you need a lesson in how not to be a traitor," I reply.

"They're a group people who also mentioned Nightmare," Randy says. "He doesn't sound like a likable guy."

"Oh…? Who did you hear that from, Keith?" I ask, suddenly interested.

"I don't know some people over there," Randy replies, pointing in the direction from which they came.

"Show me. How many people? If you're telling the truth, I shall set you free," I reply, inquisitively.

"I don't know, four or five? It was windy and dusty so I didn't get a good look at them."

"Sounds like you might come in handy after all. Let's all take a walk. Randy, Keith, Frank, let's go search for these people. I'll continue to tell you my story along the way… Once my father and Lucifer became great friends, I was ousted here to my new home. One day, when this side belongs to me, I'll force my dad and the Devil himself to dissolve their partnership. When I do, Nightmare is going to be one dead little boy. My dad will have no choice but to beg for my forgiveness. I'll run Heaven and people will worship at my feet. My father will beg, and I'll make Lucifer burn. I'll walk into the dirtiest water and he'll kiss my feet. They can't win against me; nobody can win against me, because I'm smart. When you help me catch these people, I will believe you are on my side. Do you remember what they looked like?" I ask.

"One was wearing pajamas, and another was wearing a suit from the hotel," Randy replies. "The other three were almost wearing something invisible but I can't say for sure."

"Well, you better hope we find them or I'll make an example out of you," I howl, peering at them.

"All I can tell you is what I know."

"You don't understand, Randy. I need to know where they are now. Where are they?" I shout, demandingly.

Keith and Randy point to a crevice in some debris and Randy replies, "right over there, Lord. The collapsed room."

"Show me. Do you mean this one, Randy?"

"Yes, that's the one."

"Go check it out. You had better hope they are in there. I don't like having my time wasted on stupid games," I exclaim.

"There's nobody in there, Jesus."

"Well, Randy, I guess a lesson must be learned here. Do you know what happens to people who deceive their savior? The sins they create by deceiving me must be paid," I howl.

"I didn't deceive you, Lord," Randy begs. "They were there a while ago. I swear it on my life. Two women and three men. I can't..."

"LIES! You said they were here and there is nobody in there. You will pay for your lies with your life. Nobody tricks me and gets away with it. You'll feel a new pain. A pain so great you'll be free of your lies. Have you heard of the balance of time? You'll spend your life learning the pain of time. I'll watch as you suffer," I shout.

"Please Lord, have mercy."

"My son... my mercy ends with a lie. You will know the true agony of my wrath

"I did not lie, they were in there. Please believe me!"

"I did believe you. I gave you the opportunity to bring the evil to me... instead you bring me lies. Now I must show you what these lies get you!"

I grab his arms, and Randy soon realizes he is about to come face-to-face with agonizing pain worse than death itself. Trying to fight me, Gabriel raises him above his head and smashes Randy's back onto the short point of the broken pole, impaling him midway.

His screams of pain are heard throughout the wastelands. I tie sacks to his arms and legs and fill them with sand to increase the weight.

"MY LORD, WHY?" Randy screams.

"You know why, Randy. Lying is an unforgivable sin. Considering I am generous, I will forgive you for your lies. You'll know when you are free of sin because you'll feel no more pain." I shout.

Keith and Frank run over to Randy and try to push him up.

"Stop it, Jesus! What kind of Lord are you?" Keith yells at me.

"I am a loving Lord, but Randy must pay for his sins. Which of you two would like to join him? Cut their feet off and cut their hands-off," I shout, laughing.

"Why… why are you doing this to us?" Keith asks.

"Ah, Keith. You see, I don't believe you were being honest with me…" I exclaim.

"You're not Jesus, Jesus cares about people."

Frank's screams first as Gabriel brings his sword just above Frank's ankles and severs his right foot, and then his left, with two flawless strikes. As he falls to the ground, Gabriel swings once again severing Frank's right forearm cleanly off.

"Please Jesus, have mercy on us…" Keith screams

"I do have mercy, but only for the righteous," I state.

Before Gabriel can turn again, Keith grabs Gabriel's arm and holds him from swinging again. Coming up behind Keith, Daniel sticks Keith with a knife in the back; a scream echoes as loud as the winds blowing. Gabriel swings and cuts Frank's left forearm cleanly

114

off below the elbow. The pair then turn their attention to Keith. Daniel cuts Keith's hands off slowly, while Gabriel swings his sword cutting both of Keith's legs off just below the knee with one strike.

Once Randy and Keith can no longer run away, a rope snakes up through both of Randy's shoulders, creating a noose. Randy looks like a scarecrow with a noose hanging from either side. The one is looped around Frank's chest, and the other around Keith's. Gabriel thrusts his sword through Frank's arms and pulls the rope through each of the slits, knotting them together. He then repeats this with Keith. Screams of pain, echo through the wastelands.

"You aren't the Lord!" Keith shouts.

"I am the Lord, Keith, but now do you see why you don't hide the truth from your savior? The scales have returned, and balance is restored once more, Gabriel. Let's go find the others," I reply, angrily watching as they sway in the wind, screaming in agony.

"Once you die you will be forgiven of all your sins," I tell them, grinning, as we start walking. Their screams of merciless pain echo behind us. I try to find their footprints as we go, but with the winds blowing, any trace of their tracks has long since disappeared.

"Gabriel, which way would you go if you were trying to get away?" I ask.

"If I were trying to escape, I guess that would depend," he replies, looking around. "If I heard the screams and was frightened, I would head west. If I didn't, I would have headed towards where we were, or I would head towards the most noticeable structure, the arches."

Perry Pankratz

"Yes, good point. I would assume they heard the scream and that is why those men came to aide him. We will continue west and perhaps we will meet up with the others," I reply, continuing west, listening for any noise that may divulge their location to us.

A sad day for the children.

Passing through the Arches, everything clears up. The winds cease to blow the sand, and the only noises come from the building.

"Okay, remember girls, you must be quiet. We want to surprise them. If you see anyone coming towards us you go up against the wall, okay?" I explain, looking at each of them.

"Yes, Peter. Where are we going exactly?" Emma asks.

"Well, Emma, we are going to see a couple of people. With your help, we will destroy the evil ones," I answer, putting my hand on her shoulder.

"The buildings over here aren't like those other ones," Denise notes, looking around at our surroundings.

"Well Denise, they left the building standing on this side, so they could use them for their own purposes. That's why the lights are brighter over here and there's no wind blowing. The buildings mass the people who come over. You never want to go to that place." I reply.

"What do you mean they mass the people?" Denise asks.

"Well Denise, that place is where you will either have to work for them, or they will punish you there. That's a place you do not want to go. We're going to that big tall building. The one with fire and light on it," I respond.

"That's a big building. Who's in there?" Amy asks.

"The people who made me who I am today. I was just like you kids, and then my life changed before my eyes. You know where you came from? The living world? That's a world where you can do what you want. I came from the same place, but now I can't do whatever I want. I know you're probably feeling scared right now, but I have been waiting for some help to defeat them, Amy. Today, with your help, I'll have my freedom once again," I answer, trying to hold back the hate.

"What do you mean by that, Peter? I thought you were free," Amy looks confused.

"No Amy, I'm not free. I was free when I was alive, but then the ones in that building enslaved me. Finally, I have a way to become free once again. That's why you four are here to help me. You see, you are going to gain me my freedom from these tyrants, and you four are my ticket out of here," I exclaim, staring at the building.

"What do you mean? I thought we were here to help you kill someone," Carol chimes in.

"Oh, you are Carol. I just mean you're going to help me become free again. Together, we are going to crush them. They'll die, and freedom will reign once more. You just make sure you girls keep your rocks. You don't want to drop those. We're almost to the building and that's when you're going to have to be sneaky. We have to go all the way up to the top floor without them seeing us. If they see us, we'll have to fight them too. The ones on the top floor are the ones that we need to kill. The monsters will surrender once Ged is dead," I state, smiling.

"Are you sure this is going to work Peter?" Emma asks, fear in her eyes.

"I'm as sure as I can be, Emma. There's always a chance it won't work, but together we'll win," I explain, trying to be confident.

As we continue walking through utopia, I keep looking at the children's faces. They're so innocent and pure. We finally reach the golden doors and run inside as they slide open.

"Okay," I state. "We're going to go to the back elevator at the end of the hall. Let's go. Keep up, Emma, we're almost there."

We stop at an elevator that looks like a demon. The girls are shaking, fearing what's going to happen next.

"Okay, Denise, Carol, Amy, and Emma. I'm proud of you girls. Your courage will thrust death into the monster's hearts. We'll be getting on an elevator that'll carry us to the floor below the top level. We'll have to cross a room, and then there'll be a set of stairs. Everyone ready?" I ask, looking at them all.

"Yes, I am. Why do these doors look so mean?" Emma asks in a whisper, shivering.

"They look that way to scare people from entering. Let's go and remember to be quiet. We don't want the centurions to notice us," I answer, quietly, as we creep along the side of the brimstone hallway to the elevator.

"Everyone good?" I ask, calmly.

"As good as we can Peter," Amy answers, looking afraid now.

"I know, Amy," I state, placing my palm on the eye of the demon. Within a few moments, the beast's mouth opens, and I scurry the kids in, quickly. I put my palm on the eye again until the beast's mouth closes. As the elevator growls to life and starts moving, I can see the look on the kids' faces. They look scared, so I try to talk and ease their minds.

"We'll be okay. Once these doors open, I want you to grab each other's hands. Then I want you to close your eyes and don't open them. I mean it; do not open your eyes. I'll tell you when you can open your eyes, and make sure not to let go of anyone's hands, no matter what. I'll be holding Denise's hand. Are you ready to do this?" I ask, trying to be comforting.

"I think so. What's that smell?" Denise asks.

"That's the smell of death. Don't worry about that smell; just keep your mind focused on why we're here. Don't answer any questions, just sit there and let me talk. Make sure you have those rocks I gave you too. Don't drop them," I remind them.

"We got them with us. When are we going to help you?" Emma asks.

"When I say so, I want you to stand up and just stare at them. Then when I say do it, I want you four to bring out those rocks and hold them in your hands, but don't let them be seen. Don't put them down, just hold them. Do you understand?" I reply, hoping they do.

Denise nods.

"Good. We have one chance at this, and if you fail, I fail as well. So, let's make sure we don't fail. Put this cotton in your ears so you don't hear what's going on around you," I continue, trying to make sure everything is perfect.

"We won't fail you, Peter. What's going to happen?"

"Don't worry about that. Now, grab each other's hands and don't let go. As soon as this door opens, close your eyes. Everyone holding hands?" I ask.

"Yes…" Amy starts to reply.

Just as Amy finishes saying that, the mouth of the elevator begins to open. I look to make sure their eyes are all closed, and they are. I lead the way as we make our way out of the elevator. The scourges of Hell are eating the souls of those who are tortured here. A few of them turn and look at the children and me as we walk by. The screams of people who are still alive echo through the building.

"What the hell are you doing here, Nightmare?" Michael yells.

"I finally got four children, all female. I am taking them to our Masters," I reply, annoyed.

"I'll let you pass if you leave me one of them," Michael responds, getting in our way.

"You'll let me pass or you'll pay, Michael. You know you'll go through your own trials. They've wanted four young women for years. You can have one the next time I find a girl," I state.

"You still owe me one, Nightmare," Michael points at me, shouting. "Tell me why I shouldn't call in that favor now."

"Michael, you know what happened to me the last time I gave you one. I endured the tenth level; I am not going to experience the eleventh for you. You can just sit here and wait," I shout, angrily.

"You're lucky those two upstairs like you. Otherwise I would rip your guts out and force them down your throat, Nightmare."

"Oh yes, I'm shaking. You'd be sucking my lollipop long before that would ever happen. Don't you remember what happened the last time you wanted to fight? I remember someone ended up bleeding on the floor, and it wasn't me. You can wait for the next set, why don't you go back and start gnawing on some more souls to feed your hunger? These young women belong to them, so get out of the way," I reply, smiling.

"You should be shaking, Nightmare. I won't fall for that same trick twice. Next time you will be the one sucking my lollipop."

"Don't bet on that, Michael. If I were you, I would just go back there and shut my mouth while I was ahead," I answer, confidently.

"Fine, just remember who rules this floor. Next time come alone, and we'll see who the scum is," Michael concedes.

"Anytime Michael, anytime. Now, move it," I shout, staring him down. We start walking a little faster, and just as we get to the stairs, the angel Peril stops us.

"What do we have here, Nightmare?" He asks, almost drooling.

"A gift for the Masters," I answer, annoyed.

"I'll take them from here, Nightmare. You know you are not welcome up there," Peril replies, looking between the girls and me.

"Yeah, I believe that… not! You're not taking them anywhere, Peril. These girls are my ticket out of Hell, so I'll be personally delivering them myself," I shout angrily.

"Oh, Nightmare. How I do detest you and your snide little remarks. You will only pass if I allow you to."

"You holy fools are all the same. You always want something you never deserve. Michael wants a young girl for his own greed, now you want to be the one who takes them upstairs for what reason? Could it be so you are rewarded? What other reason might there be?" I ask, staring him down.

"I want you to get down on your hands and knees and lick my feet. Then, after you're done that, I want you to look me in the eyes and tell me I'm better than you. Do you think you could do that, you piece of slime?"

"I could do that, but I won't do that for you. I'd rather just wait here and see what the Masters have to say when they see me standing here with their gifts. My guess is you'll get treated just like Jesus did. I know you wouldn't enjoy that much," I respond, cracking a smile.

"You'll pay dearly, Nightmare… You already talked to them, didn't you?" Peril responds, narrowing his eyes.

"I did. I'm not that stupid. Every time I have to bring them someone, you and your cronies are always here to stop me from doing my job. I'm sure they offered the job to you way before me, anyways. Why didn't you take it?" I ask.

"They didn't offer the job, Nightmare. I am beneath God's glory."

"Well, then I guess you know why I have to do my job as well. I'm not from Heaven, and I sure as hell am not from Hell. When they brought me here, they told me what I'd be doing and it made me sick to my stomach, but I do my job," I shout.

"You do your job all right, that's a laugh," Peril answers, with a smirk. "How many times have you gotten levels, Nightmare? Let's see if I can remember. Oh yes, ten times already. I cannot wait until you reach the thirteenth level. I'll watch you suffer the fate of a billion people. I'll enjoy watching you be shredded by all the authorities of good and evil. I'll even sit with you, every once in a while, and watch that agonizing pained look on your face. I might even join in and help them tear you apart, molecule by molecule. So yes, I am here to stop you whenever I can. Unfortunately, this time you were smart and called ahead. Therefore, you may pass this time, but next time I'll end you like I did on your seventh punishment. I did enjoy watching you suffer for that month. Take care, Nightmare. I'll be looking out for you."

"You think you're so smart, Peril, but the problem is that all of you angels are so full of yourselves and can't see that other people are just as smart as you are. I'll pay you back, and when I do I'll laugh as hard as you did watching me go through that. I'll be back down this way soon; I hope you're here waiting for me. I'd love to kick your head in again."

"Next time I'll gouge your eyes out, and you can look at the world with blind eyes. You'll be Jesus' next victim."

"Oh, that reminds me. Jesus said he can't wait for you to suck his lollipop again," I reply.

"Liar. I don't listen to Jesus and I haven't seen him since he was ousted from here."

"Well, that's what he said. If you want to go ask him yourself, he was waiting just outside the arches for one of you to come by. I had better get these gifts up to them. As always, it was your pleasure talking to me. I must go now."

"I will get you, Nightmare, and when I do, the Masters are not going to save your soul. I will make sure your soul is eternally doomed."

"Promises. Promises. I yearn for the day that your mouth quits spilling crap out of it," I reply, knowing he'll be put in his place once again.

"One day they aren't going to care about you… that's when you will die at my hands!"

I shake my head as Peril moves aside, and we head up the rounded staircase. Once we get to the top of the stairs, I place my hands over Denise's ears and pull out the cotton before doing the same for the other three. In a quiet voice I state, "Okay, open your eyes."

"That's a rotten smell down there. Why did we have to stop, Peter?" Denise asks.

"We had to get by a few evil people first. I made sure nothing happened to you then, and I'm going to make sure nothing happens to you now. We are going to go through these big gold doors now, and I need you all to stay quiet. Not one-word, okay? Do you understand?"

"I understand, but what if they ask us something?" Denise counters.

"Do not say anything. No matter what. I don't care if they ask you your name, just keep your mouth closed. Let me do all the talking and we'll be okay. Don't scream when you see them either. They aren't human, so try to prepare yourself."

There is a murmur of responses and nodding heads, so I continue.

"We have one chance, Denise. Take a deep breath to relax, and whatever you do, do not say anything. Close your eyes if you have to. Ready? Here we go," I finish, as we walk over to the door. I push the doors open, and we step inside.

What the hell is happening here?

"Frank, are you in here? Frank?" I shout, walking into room 14 with a gun and flashlight in hand. I head to the bathroom and look inside. "Frank? Where are you, Frank?" I whisper in a low tone, walking over to the shower slowly. I see Frank's kit on the floor, open. Looking inside, there's a little spoon lying on the gray sand.

"Has anyone seen Frank Ortiz?" I ask, walking out of the room again.

"You mean the forensic guy?" An officer responds.

"Yes, have you seen him?"

"No, I haven't seen him since he went in there."

"Oh crap, not again. Sam, I think Frank went through the wall with the other two officers."

"You got to be kidding me," Same replies, looking stunned. "Jesus Christ. Close off the room until we find someone who knows what the hell is going on."

"Yes, sir. Stay back people," I shout, closing the door and putting tape across it. I head to the lobby, looking back just as a woman comes out of her room.

"Please people, go back to your rooms," I say for what feels like the hundredth time.

I watch the woman go back inside and close the door behind her before I continue to the lobby. Joining a few more officers, we stand there trying to figure out what happened. Our opinions and theories are far out there, and nothing is making sense.

An older woman approaches the desk and asks, "Where's Amanda tonight? Was she that tired that she left early?"

"No Edna," Vanessa replies, "four girls and Amanda disappeared in room 14 tonight. From what I've heard, three officers are also missing."

"Are you kidding?"

"No, Edna, I'm not."

"Oh, that's terrible. We've been trying to figure out ourselves what's going on in that room with all the disappearances..."

"Excuse me," I interrupt, "did you say there were more disappearances from that room?"

"Yes, officer. Amanda said there's a book in the office with people who left their luggage behind. Most of those people stayed in 14."

"Would I be able to see that book?" I ask.

"I guess? Amanda left the office door open when she went to check the room for the missing kids. I'll see if I can find it," Vanessa answers, looking puzzled.

"Thank you, Miss. What else can you tell me about room 14?" I ask, turning back to Edna.

"Well, the big clue is that every time someone disappears, there's grayish colored sand left in the shower."

"Do you know how much? I'm asking because there's about seven or eight inches of it right now sitting in the bathroom," I continue, trying to determine how many people have gone missing.

"It's never been that much. I know what I cleaned out of there was half an inch at best, and just in one little spot."

"Alright. Any other strange events that you can think of?" I ask, trying to scrape for answers.

"I'm sorry, officer. There's nothing that I can remember offhand. I know Amanda and I were talking about spirits, but I don't think that's what you want to hear."

"That's what we're going on ourselves. I know it sounds funny, but considering nothing else makes sense…" I answer.

"Yes, Amanda and I also discussed the number thirteen. I know thirteen has unexplained phenomena associated with it. I learned from Amanda that they changed it to fourteen years ago, but that room is the thirteenth apartment."

"Yes, I know, my family is superstitious against thirteen as well. They will avoid it at all costs. That explains a lot, Edna," I respond.

"When I was a little young girl, my mom stepped on a man's grave. To make a long story short, mom had to make a blood sacrifice to this man on his grave. After mom had made the sacrifice, that pleased him, and he quit haunting her. I don't know if this will help, but it did work for her."

"Okay, so who would we call in to correct this if we needed someone?" I ask.

"I don't know who to call. Perhaps someone who deals with spirits?"

"That's a good idea; I'll talk to my sergeant in a moment here. Thank you again for all your help."

"No problem, officer. Anything I can do to help."

"Excuse me, officer?" Vanessa gets my attention. "I think I may have found that ledger."

"Thank you. May I take a look at it for a moment?" I ask, smiling.

"You may, but please be careful. My boss will fire me if it is gone."

"I'll keep it right here. Are all these ones from room 14?" I ask, looking at the entries.

"No... the ones in the red are from fourteen, the others are in blue. Some of the entries show that they've contacted us about their items. It shows the room numbers as well."

"Okay, I see it now. I'm not familiar with how hotels mark their stolen or lost items."

"The stolen items are checked differently, and immediately reported to the police. When it comes to luggage or miscellaneous items, they're reviewed in this book. This way, when the person calls we can figure out quickly where their items are."

"Oh, I see. That makes sense. Sergeant, come here for a second," I shout, turning away from Vanessa.

"What's up, officer?"

"This room has a history. There have been at least forty times where someone's luggage has been forgotten or left behind," I state.

"Holy. Why weren't we told?"

"I'm not sure officer?" Vanessa cuts in. "Just by the handwriting, I can say it's been over the span of a few years. There have only been one or two managers that would've been here longer, and they're gone now. These entries were all one person, but the last 12 pages are from different managers."

"Okay yes, I see that now. I don't know why those managers didn't report this to us. That's several people who've left their luggage behind and just disappeared. That's at least thirty people right there," I count, puzzled.

"That's why Amanda and I were trying to figure out what was going on," Edna joins the conversation. "She realized there was something weird about that room, but she couldn't find anything to take to you yet."

"Don't worry, we weren't thinking about charging Amanda with this. What is your name is…?" I ask, looking at the worried look forming across her face.

"People just call me Edna. I work in housekeeping here."

"Okay, Edna. Thank you again for your help with trying to figure out what's going on in room 14. Sergeant, I'm going to run the names of these people and see what comes up, all right?"

"Go ahead. Let me know as soon as you have the information back."

"Do you mind if I take the book to that seat over there?" I ask Vanessa.

"That's fine."

I walk over and sit down and open the book up as I begin calling in the names of the people who had disappeared from the hotel. About half an hour later, my radio crackles to life. It's dispatch.

"All of the names you have listed have missing persons cases filed."

"Thank you dispatch, 10-4 over," I respond, standing up and heading over to the desk to return the ledger to Vanessa.

"Did you find anything helpful?" She asks.

"Actually, I did. It seems all the names except the last few are all listed as missing persons," I respond, sternly.

"Oh my God, really?" Vanessa asks, looking shocked.

"Yes, I would make it a policy to contact police whenever someone disappears from here in the future," I respond, curtly, walking away.

Walking away is hard to do.

The winds continue to blow as move away from the screams of agony coming from the two officers and the mysterious third person. As we continue to trudge through these godforsaken sands, I can't help but wonder. *"How many people have come through that wall and been in the same place I am standing now? Their lives ruined because they were just there."* Looking over at David, his face is worn with time, and he's wrapped in a sheet that has been almost sandblasted away in these conditions.

"How did you know Jesus was going to be there?" I ask, breaking the silence.

"I didn't," David responds, looking at me with sadness. "I've just been around long enough to know that if there's a commotion he'll come see what is happening. I'm sorry I got snippy with you two back there, Amanda."

"You weren't, and you saved our lives," I reply, more understandingly.

"Yes, I did, but I shouldn't have been rude about it. I do apologize for it."

"What would happen if we passed through those arches?" I ask, inquiringly.

David looks shocked, as if I've flipped my lid for asking. Taking a deep breath he explains, "Well, you'd have the armies of Heaven and Hell, and who knows what waiting behind them for you."

"Are there any hiding places by the arches? I mean close enough to see?" I ask, trying to gain some knowledge.

"I believe there is. Why? What are you thinking?"

"I think if nothing else, why don't I check out what's going on there. What's the worst that could happen? I find something out that will help us? I'm tired of running, and honestly, I would rather stand up and take something on the chin," I respond, thinking.

"That's commendable, Amanda. Are you sure you would want to do something like that and risk your life?"

"Yes, truthfully I do. My whole life I've never run away from as many challenges as I've run away from here, David. I want to stand up and spit in the eye of these mongrels. If I'm going to die for something, I'll die standing my ground," I reply, confidently.

"I do understand your point, Amanda, but there's still Jesus to contend with, too. He's a scavenger and I'm sure he will find us hiding around there."

"I don't care anymore. All my life I have stood there and taken whatever has come my way. I may not be living anymore, but I am sure as hell not going to stand here as a bunch of crusaders try to make death a living hell for everyone. With luck, I'll even find those children that went missing. I don't know about you four, but I sure as hell am going to give it a try. Win or die," I shout.

"Okay, Amanda. You've got me on board. What do you say, should we make one last stand for all the marbles?" I address our companions.

Ray shakes his head and responds, "sure, what the hell. I'm with you, Amanda."

"As long as you know what you're doing, Amanda, I'll follow you," Frank adds.

Debbie looks around and answers,

"It's about time we do something," Debbie chimes in. "I'll follow you down, Amanda. My husband's already dead; I have nothing left to lose."

"Okay then, let's go make some noise and wreck their bliss," I exclaim, looking at everyone. We turn towards the arches, and make our way through the entanglement of debris, trying to stay hidden. We listen for voices and can still hear the screams of the officers in the distance.

We finally reach the arches a few hours later, and sit at a distance, watching them. I can hear moaning, and it doesn't seem to be coming from the officers.

"What the hell? What is that moaning? Where is it coming from?" I whisper.

"I don't know, but it's coming from over there. I'm guessing it's one of Jesus' captures," Ray responds.

"Do you think we should go check it out?" I ask, uncertain.

"Well, what would you say, Amanda? This is your expedition, so it's your decision."

"I say we can use all the help we can get. What's the worst that could happen, right?" I mutter.

"You don't want me to answer that do you, Amanda?" David asks, eyeing me.

"No, David, it was just rhetorical. Let's go find out who this one is," I answer.

As we make our way to the other side of the archway, I keep looking back to make sure no one is coming out, and that Jesus isn't coming our way. We finally make our way into where the moaning is coming from, and we all prepare for a fight. Peeking around the corner, I see one man hanging, and look to see if there is anyone else.

"Okay, there is just one person in there, let's go," I whisper, quietly, as we all head inside.

"BRAD!" Debbie screams upon seeing the victim.

David looks around and checks to see if anyone is coming. He turns back and whispers, "is that your husband, Debbie?"

"Yes, that's her husband," I answer, looking at the shape he is in

"Oh, Brad, what have they done to you?" Debbie wails.

"Debbie. Please help me. I'm in pain," Brad moans in a faint voice.

Ray examines at each spike, a pained look comes over his face as he states.

"Sorry to say this, Brad, but you're going to be in a lot more pain when we're finished getting these spikes out."

"Oh, Brad. I thought I'd never get to see you again," Debbie sobs.

"I never thought I'd get to see you either, my love. Why did you lead me here?"

"It wasn't me!" Debbie answers, looking confused. "I swear it wasn't. I'm here because of someone called Nightmare. He told me to run to the west. Wait! He told me he was going to have to take you through the arches. That's where I ran into these three. And Amanda of course."

"Yes, what are you doing here Amanda?"

"That's a long story. If we make it, I'll tell you the whole tale," I reply, still dumbfounded by the events of the past few hours.

"Jesus did say something about Nightmare. He said I was walking with Nightmare and that they had watched me the whole time. I should've known better, Debbie. I had a dream, a dirty dream, and we were going to the shower and we fell through into here. You were so angry about the fantasy I had. I should've known you would never be that mad. I'm so sorry, Debbie."

Debbie kisses Brad on the lips, and as she pulls away, replies, "don't worry about it baby. We're together, and that's all that matters. I'm never leaving your side again, I promise."

Ray comes back with some wire that he places around the head of the spikes. As they pull, Brad's screams of pain echo loudly. David holds Brad still while we pull the other spikes out of his hands, and once they're all removed, he falls to the ground.

"How do we heal his hands?" I ask, concerned as I watch Brad writhe on the ground. His howls are wolf-like, and hard to listen to. Ray stands up and comes over to me.

"That's the problem," he says. "It'll take time to heal. With no power, everything takes ten times longer. I'm guessing Debbie will want to stay here with Brad?"

"Are you going to stay here, Debbie, or are you coming with us to help make our stand?" I ask.

Debbie looks at each one of us, and her tears tell us everything we need to know. "I'm going to stay here with Brad. He needs me right now."

"No, Debbie. You go take care of that son of a bitch. I'll be here waiting for you when you're victorious. Listen Debbie, I love you and I love that you have found me and vowed to remain beside me, but there are bigger fish to deal with right now. I will only hold you back. I am not going to be responsible for anyone's death. You go help them; give them everything you have. I'll be here waiting, proud of you. There are only five of you, but five is better than four. I'll be with you, in your heart, as you beat down whatever you go up against. I love you, now go."

"I love you, Brad. I promise I'll be back for you."

"I know you will baby," Brad says, mustering a smile and taking a deep breath. "I'll be waiting right here for you when you get back. I love you."

"We had better get going now," David interrupts says, interrupting the pair.

"Yes, David, let's go," Debbie says coldly, her eyes filling with tears.

The curse of 13

The five of us head out of the building and back to our hiding spot, close to the arches. We continue to sit there, watching and waiting, hoping to catch a glimpse of people moving around on the other side.

"Okay here's what I'm going to do," I say, breaking the silence. "I'm going to head through those arches, and if you follow me I want you to hide somewhere. If anything happens to me I don't want you to be captured, okay?"

Ray looks at me, shaking his head as he replies, "okay, Amanda, are you sure you want to do this?"

"I'm as sure as I am ever going to be," I answer, trying to smile at the others.

"Okay, I'll follow you then. Let us know if you find any weapons."

"If I find anything, you'll be the first to know. I'll see you on the other side." I state, taking a deep breath before standing and making a mad dash for the arches.

I look over my shoulder briefly as I run faster than I ever thought possible. I see the arches before me and stop, hiding behind a rock. I try to peer inside, but can't see anything, so I take a deep breath and run through to the other side.

Perry Pankratz

In the Kingdom of Helleven

As the door slams shut behind us, we approach the two thrones at the far end of the room. I can see both Lucifer and God with their demented smiles as they look towards the children. The echoes from our footsteps sound as if there is an army behind us. A fire that burns between their thrones is the only light source in the room, and their shadows dance on the walls. We keep walking until the floor turns from black to red. We kneel down, and I keep my eyes fixated on the pair.

"Ah, Nightmare. Great to see you again. What gifts do you bring us this time?"

"Isn't it obvious, Lucifer? Nightmare has some brought us these girls," God exclaims, clasping his hands together.

"I can see that. I assume you want something in exchange for this gift?"

"He's already on his tenth level of pain. I'm sure he wants us to bring him down to level three or four?" God suggests.

"I do want something from you both, but I don't care what level I'm on. I put up with your moron angels and idiotic demons making comments all the time…" I shout, sternly.

"Watch your tongue boy," God warns me. "You'll find yourself put through level eleven if you don't."

"I don't care, God. You see, I've come to realize that without me, you would never get these people here. I've been bringing people to you both for over a hundred and thirty years. I've gifted you the young and old. I think I deserve a hell of a lot more respect from you and your armies. On my way up here with these girls, I had Michael and Peril both try to steal them away. Every time I come here, those two scavengers are always there saying or doing something," I shout.

"They watch out for us. They ensure our safety," God argues.

"Who are you afraid of? Who's going to attack this place? Nobody has ever crossed the arches and nobody will. The only one that comes to this dwelling is me. Therefore, I ask you again… why are they really here, God?" I demand.

"You better listen up, Nightmare. Yes, you bring us people, but you are bordering on something that's better not said. You're right, nobody has ever made it to the top floor other than you, but that doesn't mean Jesus won't try to make his way back up here again."

"Jesus is a scavenger in the wastelands, God. You know he cannot make it back through those arches unless you allow him too. Nobody in the wastelands has passed through those arches unless I was escorting them. I have been loyal and done everything you have said to do. I think I deserve a spot above the riffraff. If you only gave me a little power, I'd be able to bring more people here for you both. I think these four children are worth that at least," I demand, confidently.

Lucifer looks at me, his eyes fixed as if he is trying to figure something out. A few moments later, he shouts, "it looks like our little Nightmare is growing up a bit. So, you want to barter these children for extra luxuries?"

"I do, my Lord. I think that's the least I deserve."

"If I had a kid like you, I'd slap the crap out of you, and make you feel real pain," God intervenes. "Then I would put you through so much for trying to blackmail me into doing what you want. How dare you even consider trying that after everything we've given you?"

"What do you mean everything you've given me? You disrespect me as much as your angels and demons do. For over one hundred and thirty years, I have gifted you people without power. Do you not realize, by now, that I could bring you three times the people with power? You both keep telling me how you want to end this world. I have worked one room for the last twenty years and I've gifted you so many people. More rooms could use thirteen. There are so many thirteens out there to use; you know in your hearts I'm telling the truth." I shout.

"Shut your mouth for a second, Nightmare. If I hear one more word out of your lips, I'll slap you so hard," God interrupts.

They lean towards the middle, and their whispers are barely audible. I turn and look at the girls to see that they are frightened, so I try to reassure them with my eyes. Two of them seem to recognize that I mean them no harm, but the other two are looking more afraid by the second. I go back to looking at God and Lucifer who are still huddled behind the fire. After a few minutes, they sit up in their own thrones.

God looks at me, his eyes hardened with hate, as he speaks. "You say you've done so much for us, but yet you are on your tenth level pain. What do you think that tells us about you?"

"In the beginning I did not like having to do that. I let those first four go because I did not understand. I also had Michael telling me I had to give him the people I caught since my fifth level pain. You said I had to listen to the angels and demons, and I took the punishment for what they told me to do. Peril does the same. He wants everyone I bring. Since the last time, I have made sure you have gotten everyone I have brought. I have not received a new level in over twenty years. I think that says a lot about me, don't you think?" I demand, standing straight up.

"I believe that you've got a mouth on you," God counters. "Yes, you have made significant mention of Michael and Peril and the multitude of demons you say are responsible for taking these people. However, I think you're just soft hearted and let them go in the wastelands."

"Why would I let them go into the wastelands? Jesus is your son, isn't he? He would torture and maul any person in the wastelands. It makes no sense to me let them waste out there," I shout, annoyed.

"Look, Nightmare. Do you know the reason we decided there should be no Heaven and Hell? I'll tell you why. Those human feces factories are always whining about what they want and what they need. There is only so much crap we can put up with. Ministers and preachers take money that's intended for me. They are stealing from me and using it for their own greed. They need to be removed from the world. That's why you are here, Nightmare. That is the only reason you are still living today. We need someone who will bring us these living souls."

Lucifer looks at me, his eyes cold and heartless as he shouts.

"Yes," Lucifer adds, "as God said, there comes a time when you've had enough of people selling their souls for something that equals nothing. By joining together, we no longer need to indulge these human beings anymore. They will get no more than what we decide they'll get. They want salvation? We'll give them salvation. Once they get here, they realize quickly that their salvation is not what they expected. You see, Nightmare, we have a great plan here. There is no longer an in between. They can cry and whine all they want about Heaven and Hell, but once they get here we can make them do whatever we want. You want power? How much power are you looking for, Nightmare?"

"I want enough so I don't have to keep coming up with new and improved ploys to get people to follow me. In the beginning, getting people to the wastelands was a breeze. Now, trying to get into these people's heads is much more difficult. I don't think I'm asking a lot and think that's a fair trade with what I've brought you here today," I shout.

"Lucifer and I agree on many things," God starts. "We agree human beings should all die and come here as soon as possible. Hell, Lucifer and I even agree that all people should suffer at our hands.

The curse of 13

For too long we have allowed people to dictate what we do, and now they are slowly learning we've had enough. I don't agree that you should have power, though. I think you should continue doing things the way you've been doing them since you started."

"I could do it the same way, but I guarantee you're going to be waiting a lot longer than you figure for more souls. The curse of thirteen is only going to last so long, and then I'll have to figure out another place and time to get these people to you. What you don't understand fully is that humans have tendencies to think, sometimes rationally, sometimes irrationally. Your problem is going to be when they figure out people are disappearing. They'll get smart, and they'll close that whole place off. It might take years to find another thirteen door to the living world. You want people here now, I can only bring people when I can get them. Giving me power would enable me to create new doors and create a panic. See, these humans scare easy, but they also regroup and think rationally. If I create new doors, which attach to anything thirteen, I'll have a whole new curse," I explain.

"You talk about this thirteen as a curse, why?" Lucifer asks, rubbing his chin.

"Well, Master, people are afraid of the number thirteen. I have seen people doing everything they can to make sure there are no thirteens. How long do you believe it will be before I can no longer open a door to their world?" I exclaim.

"Perhaps Nightmare has a point," Lucifer says, thoughtfully. "Humans are easily fooled, but they may become wise to our game."

"Honestly, once people start realizing that thirteen is the worst of the worst, they'll try anything to rid the world of it. If they have thirteen books they might throw one away, but as long as there are 12 books on a desk it still equals thirteen. Thirteen houses in a row? I can still get them. But without the power to open these doors, all that is useless. You say you want humankind dead, and I say put your power where your mouth is and let me open these doors. Within months I could bring you thousands instead of three here and four there..." I shout, seeing the looks in their eyes.

"You talk a big game, Nightmare," God responds, anger in his voice. "Okay, let's say we allow you to have this power to open doors. What is our guarantee you won't try to escape or try to create your own utopia?"

"What the hell do I care about a utopia? Why would I escape if I have nothing in the living world anymore?" I yell.

"Yes, but you are angry, and I think your anger is directed at us," God continues.

"No. My anger is at your son, Jesus. He can't touch me when I have people with me, but he is a nuisance always running around with his weapons," I shout, glaring at them.

God looks mortified as he bellows, "weapons? What weapons? He's in the wastelands with nothing."

"That is where you are wrong. Your demons and angels are passing off weapons to him. I've had to dodge spears, swords, and a multitude of other weapons," I shout.

Lucifer and God lean in towards each other again, and I can barely make out the occasional audible word. I keep an eye on the pair, watching them behind the flames discussing. After about 15 minutes, they finally return to their seats.

"We still don't agree on giving you power, but I will offer you a challenge," God states, glaring at me. "If you kill one of my son's companions, I will concede and agree with Lucifer to give you some power. If you do not succeed with this challenge, there will not be an eleventh or twelfth level…you will go straight to the thirteenth. Do you accept this challenge, Nightmare?"

"I will agree to this challenge on one condition, these kids come with me. I know you too well. When I get back you will have mutilated and done something horrendous to them," I shout, looking at the children.

"Are you questioning our integrity?" God shouts.

"I am not questioning your integrity, I'm questioning your honor and what comes out of your mouths. These four young girls will be the same in twenty-four hours as they are now," I reply.

"How do you intend to kill one of Jesus' guards with four children there?" God asks, his gaze fixed on the girls. "You won't be able to do it. Leaving the children with us is your best bet."

"God has a point there, Nightmare," Lucifer adds. "How can you possibly kill in front of these innocent children? I wouldn't want to have to hurt you if their skin is damaged in any shape or form."

"As you have mentioned to me, many times before, but I'll take my chances. These children are my guarantee that you'll honor what you say. If I leave them with you now, you'll just get Peril and Michael to impede my progress back here. You might even send out a few demons and whatever else to help stop me." I say.

"How dare you," God counters. "We offer you a chance to earn our love and respect and you spit in our face with accusations of what may happen? I should strike you down right where you stand."

"That was a fair deal we offered to you, Nightmare," Lucifer adds. "I could bring up a thousand demons to disembowel, or I could make you eat your insides. I can do punishments to you that would give your grandchildren nightmares. You should be kissing our feet."

"You offered me a challenge, and I gave you one condition. These girls come with me, and after I kill Jesus' companion, I'll return with them. Then they belong to you. Until then, these girls belong to me. They'll return in the same condition they are in now. That's the one condition I have, Masters. You can agree to it, or you can kill me right here and have a bigger problem later," I finish.

God glares at me, and then the girls, as he grimaces as if pondering his options. Lucifer has an evil look as if he's debating whether to have those demons come up or not. After a few minutes of staring, God finally breaks the silence.

"You must be confident, Nightmare, knowing what we can do to you and you still being defiant. I am debating with myself right now if I should strike you dead or if I should wait until you finish the challenge."

"I like the fire in your heart, but there comes a time where you should concede," Lucifer adds. "We'll get these girls either way, so I say we let him take them with him. But if there is even one hair out of place on their head, pain and agony will be your eternity. I'll personally be the one you see every day if they are harmed. Do you want to risk having to endure that for all of the eternity?"

"Of course, I wouldn't expect any less. These children are going to make sure I kill at least one of Jesus' men. There's no greater power in the world than that of a child." I exclaim.

"He does seem confident doesn't he, Lucifer?" God ponders. "I don't know, I'd still rather have them here safely with us."

"How many followers does Jesus have?" Lucifer continues.

"The last I saw, two, and they all have weapons. I can win, though," I respond.

"It's risky taking those children out there. How about this, Nightmare. What if we get a neutral person to watch the girls until you return?"

"No, thank you. I want these children near me when I slaughter your son and his guards." I reply.

"Oh? You're going to kill them all? I doubt that you will kill them all. Especially Jesus."

"Oh, I will kill them all. When I am finished I will bring what's left of them back here." I shout.

Lucifer glares at me, looking thoughtful as he leans forward, his hands propping up his head. His gaze alternates between the girls and me.

Second thoughts

Crossing through the aches and hiding behind a building, I look at all the building. It is so much different from the other side. I only have a moment to stare in awe before the rest of them follow.

"Amanda, are you sure about this?" David whispers, looking around.

"No David, I don't know about this. All I know for sure is that running isn't going to solve anything for us. If we can at least find something to use against them, we might stand a chance of living," I whisper back.

I scan each of the buildings, trying to see which would be most likely to hold the children.

"Yes, that's for sure," David mutters. "I hope we can find something good to use. This place is so weird though. There's no wind or sand blowing. I guess it's only the best for them."

"Let's make our way to that big building over there," I finally decide, hoping I am right.

"What if they're waiting for us?" David replies.

"Well, then you can blame me for screwing up. Have you noticed there's no one walking around here?"

"I did but didn't want to point it out. You know with that bad luck and all."

"I understand that, and I'm sure those devils will be around. I'll tell you what, I'll go into the building myself. That way I'm the one only one who pays if they're there waiting," I state.

"I vowed to stick with you," David argues. "Right or wrong, I'm not changing my mind now."

"I'll do whatever it takes to get you out," Ray adds. "No matter what happens, I'm here for you, Amanda."

"I want to get my husband out," Debbie whispers. "I'll do whatever I need to see that happen."

"Thank you all. I know this is a fool-hearted plan, but I just cannot run anymore. At least if we try, nobody can say we're scared of them. I am so sick of seeing people die because of this crap," I whisper angrily, but with a little more confidence.

We make our way even further in, trekking towards the building, trying to remain undetected. After running for a while, we all come to a stop, looking at the huge building. Finally, we slip inside the sliding doors and look around for any signs of movement. No one is around, and the only sound is the echo of our footsteps down the halls.

"Look at those doors," David says. "They all look like demon faces…why?"

"My guess is intimidation. Those are some of the ugliest doors I've ever seen," I whisper back.

"Yes, that could be it," Ray nods, inspecting one of the doors. "I wonder what would happen if we tried to figure out how those work?"

"I just thought about something," David interrupts, excitedly. "What if those aren't doors, but elevators with demons hiding behind them, waiting for people like us?"

"You know you might be right, David. I didn't even think about that. That would be a great way to capture people. Nobody is on guard waiting for an elevator. We should wait and see if anyone comes out?"

"That way we will know if they're safe or not," Ray agrees, nodding.

We look around for a place to hide and observe, and after a few minutes of searching, we find some rocks piled up near the far end of the hall with a clear view of the elevators. We sit waiting for hours before we finally hear some noise. Peering over the rocks, I almost fall over when I see an Angel and Demon walking together, talking.

They stop and the demon sniffs, "Dumah, do you smell human here?"

"Zozo. Probably from Nightmare bringing those children here, Zozo," the angel replies. "You never forget the smell of a baby."

The demon lets out a blood curdling laugh, "That's for sure. How I would love to look into the frightened eyes of a child again. There's nothing better than watching them leak their fluids all over the place. The crying, the begging for forgiveness and mercy. Do you remember when this was purgatory?"

"Oh yes," the angel screeches. "Those human children beg like no other. 'Oh please, don't hurt me; I'll do whatever you want.' Yes, I do remember when this was purgatory. I remember when they told us to come together and destroy it, too. They had no idea it was coming."

"The stupid looks on their faces as they watched us united as one. Oh yes, the screams of pain and asking for mercy were priceless."

The angel still laughing replies.

"I remember, this one woman had been murdered, and was just coming to grips with the idea of being dead. She thought I was there to take her to Heaven. The look on her face when I stabbed her over and over again was priceless."

"I remember that… You took her to Heaven all right. On the edge of your sword!"

"Great isn't it how a smell of children can bring back the fondest memories?"

"What do you think they're doing to those children right now?" The demon asks, sniffing again.

"Well Zozo, if I were in their spot right now, I'd be drawing out their fear. I would make them pay for everything their race has done to us," the angel responds.

"If I were there with them, I'd grab them by the sides of their heads and look them dead in the eyes as I showed them their eternity. I would draw my claws down their chests and make them beg."

"You do paint such detailed pictures, Zozo. I guess I should get back up to the second floor and continue to show these human hosts a good time."

The demon shouts out.

"Yes, today I'm on the third floor. I'm making people eat the bugs of their past."

"If we were allowed to do everything we wanted, they would only last a minute," the angel replies, chuckling.

"You got that right, Dumah," the demon responds.

We watch them as they walk to the elevator and push on the eyes. The demon's mouth opens, and the demon gets in one elevator while the angel gets in another, stopping briefly to look around as the doors close.

"Did you see that? Those are elevators. The demon went to the third floor and the angel went to the second floor. That angel walked into the second elevator from the front, and the demon walked into the one right next to it. Do you think these are set to just stop at one floor?" I whisper, hopefully.

"That's possible, Amanda," David answers me. "Hang on one second. One, two, three… there are thirteen lifts. I'm not going back outside, but I'll just assume there are thirteen floors."

"Okay. If the way they got into the elevators suggests the second and third floor, would that mean the thirteenth floor would be the elevator just on that side? I'm assuming they have the same setup as the others. I bet the thirteenth elevator leads right to God and the Devil," I think out loud, unsure of what may await us if I'm wrong.

"I'm sure they do, but let's just wait for a bit and see if anyone else comes out," David suggests. "We'll at least get an idea of what we're up against."

"I agree with you, David. The more we know, the better our odds of winning," I mutter, feeling hopeful.

We sit while demons and angels periodically come in and out of the demon mouths. Watching the figures move in and out becomes monotonous until Debbie suddenly puts her hand over her mouth and whispers, "oh my God! That's Nightmare!"

He stops short and looks around, sniffing the air. I swear he's looking right at us, but he continues walking after a moment.

"That's the one who took the kids?" I whisper, gritting my teeth in anger.

"Oh my God, he must have taken the children to the thirteenth floor," Ray gasps.

"We have to go up there and save those kids," I reply.

"We don't know what's up there and we have nothing to defend ourselves with."

"I don't care. We have to do something. I would rather die saving someone than hide here, waiting to see what's going to happen. I'll go myself," I mutter.

"No, you won't. I'll go with you," David butts in.

"You don't have to, David. This is my choice, and if I am wrong that's my own problem."

"We'll all go. We've come this far together; we might as well go the rest of the way."

Everyone nods, agreeing. Waiting a moment to gather courage, I look over at David and we stand, running to the elevator. I place my hands on the eye of the demon, waiting. The elevator stops, and the mouth opens. We check to make sure nobody is inside before cramming in. Once inside, however, nothing happens.

"The elevator isn't closing. What are we going to do?" David asks, sounding panicked.

Ray looks around and replies, "There has to be some ritual to close the door. What if we pushed the demon's eye from this side?"

"Well, it couldn't hurt to try?" I whisper, anxiously pushing on the eye.

Everyone presses on the eye after I do, and the mouth begins to close. We just stand there, looking around for a moment. Suddenly there's a jerk and we feel the movement of the elevator. With a combination of worried faces, we realize there's no turning back now.

"What're we going to do when we get up there?" David asks.

"Well, there are five of us. I say we stay in the elevator and if someone comes in, we attack them. It gives us ten fists and ten feet to beat them with," I reply, trying to think of ways to hurt them.

"I'll give you credit, that's an interesting attack," Ray laughs. "I guess we'll see what happens whenever this elevator stops."

"You three over there will stay on this side," I dictate, trying to figure some sort of strategy.

As the elevator stops I can see the fearful eagerness in everyone's eyes as we wait to see what is on the other side of the door. I press the eye and quickly move back. The mouth begins to open, and the smell of death comes wafting in. I almost throw up and have to hold my mouth closed.

"Oh god, what the hell is that?" Debbie gags.

The curse of 13

"It smells like someone died," I reply, trying to hold back from losing my lunch.

We try to remain silent as we hear screams and voices coming from outside the elevator. I peer around the corner, and an angel catches my attention. He is dragging someone across the floor, and I quickly duck back behind the door to avoid being seen. I peer out again and make sure the coast is clear before zipping out and around the corner, into a line of people against the wall. Everyone else soon follows me, and we sit listening as the angel speaks to these people.

"Oh come on, you like it. You love it when I put my hand on your chest and rip out your heart. Perhaps I'll stick my fingers in your eyes again. Quit your screaming, Richard, you know you like it."

We sit there, horrified, and just listen. I want to throw up with every word he says.

The second coming of Jesus

Coming down the elevator, I think to myself, *"if I find out they've touched one of those girls, I will kill them both. If I hadn't overstepped on that one comment, I could have taken them with me."*

The speaker crackles to life and God's voice states, "remember Nightmare, you must be back in 48 hours or you lose!"

"Yes, I remember. It won't take me that long; once I find them, I will kill them all!" I shout.

"Good luck with that Nightmare, my son is very cunning and will probably send your remains back to me!"

"I guess we will see about that!" I shout back. I stand there waiting until the elevator stops, and when the door begins to open, I step out. As I walk, a smell catches my attention I stop briefly to think, looking towards a pile of rocks. Unable to identify it, I turn and run out the door and into the wastelands. As I walk, I can hear a low moaning. Walking towards it, I see Brad trying to move towards the entrance.

"Who are you?" He manages to ask, in a quiet voice.

"I'm Nightmare, Brad… it looks like Jesus did a number on you. I will say, by the looks of it you got a threesome: two in the hands and one in the feet," I reply, laughing.

"YOU! You did this to me…" Brad shouts through gasps of pain.

"Brad, perhaps you should not have been in that room. I have a job to do, and now… you are going to help me. How are your lungs?" I ask, smiling.

Brad takes three deep breaths in between moaning and tries to shout, "no! I am not going to…"

Grabbing him by the throat, I pick him up. "Now Brad, I asked you nicely. I need you to scream for me… got it?"

"Yes…" he answers in a small voice.

"That's good. Doesn't it feel good to help others? Let's go for a little walk," I state. We make our way closer to the arches before I set him down again. "Come on, Brad, here you go. Scream away for me."

When he doesn't make a sound, I kick him in the hands and stomp on his feet. His resulting screams echo throughout the wastelands. Leaving him, I make my way to the top of the building to keep an eye from him and wait. Half an hour later, Jesus and one of his cronies show up.

"Well, I am impressed Brad. How did you get down from there? Nobody ever gets down alive," Jesus says.

"I bet Nightmare released him, my Lord," Gabriel says, looking around with his hand on his sword.

"No, I don't think so. I smell a woman on him and I bet it was his wife. Brad, how did you get down?"

"Nightmare..." Brad whispers, struggling to catch his breath.

"What? You're a liar, Brad. You said you don't lie, but here we are," Jesus shouts, standing up.

I listen to them speak as I sneak up to Gabriel, grab his sword quickly, and just as Jesus turns around, surprise him with a quick slice. Gabriel's sword cuts across Jesus's neck, and another cuts Gabriel down. As Jesus lays there, blood pouring out of his neck, he looks at me astonished by what is happening. Grabbing Gabriel, I slice his head off and stuff it in my bag. Turning and walking back to Jesus, the fear in his eyes shows that he knows I am going to do the same to him.

"I wish I would have killed you in Purgatory…" Jesus whispers, in a barely audible voice.

Smiling down at him, I respond, "I wish you would have too."

I take the blade and make quick work of him, also putting his head in the bag. Looking around, I see a figure running towards me that looks like Michael.

"My lord!" He calls.

He runs and falls at the Jesus' decapitated body, holding him up to his chest and crying.

Seeing the bloody sack in my hands, he turns to me. "You killed Jesus… You are going to pay, Nightmare!"

"Everyone is always saying I'll pay, but it seems to me everyone else is paying," I reply, watching him stand, hatred in his eyes.

"You are an evil little one, Nightmare. Ever since purgatory you do their bidding, and now you killed our savior. The one man who actually loved people."

"I know I'm evil, but you all made me this way. You think Jesus loved people? You've got to be kidding me. He's left more people dead along these wastelands then I have sent through those arches," I reply.

"That's only because they lied to him…"

"They didn't lie to him. Jesus wanted it to be me so bad, and he slaughtered innocent people. I left enough people on this side of the arches so that one day there would have been enough to fight God and the Devil, and he slaughtered them all." I shout.

"You sent them to kill him, don't deny it!" Daniel yells back.

"No, I didn't. I let people go to bring Purgatory back to life again. Jesus was no better than the ones over there."

"You're a liar and I have going to kill you!"

"Go ahead and try, but I have something special for you. You were there when they destroyed purgatory; you killed almost everyone there. God and the Devil created me. Yes, I have to do their bidding now, but not for long."

"What are you going to do, Nightmare? Cut my head off? Go ahead and do it then."

"No Daniel, you believed in what Jesus did. You are going beyond the arches, and you will feel my pain."

"Oh, no, I'm not going over there. I'll kill myself before that happens… better yet, I'll kill you!"

He pulls out a dagger, and looks back and forth between it and me, as if deciding how to end me.

"Accept what is going to happen to you, Daniel. I have been waiting for this moment for a long time."

"No, I am going to kill you!"

He runs at me with the dagger in front of him, but I raise my sword and strike his hand as the dagger flies by my head. He sees his hand, split in two, and looks up at me shocked.

"Why didn't you kill me?" He asks.

"I told you, you are going through those arches," I reply.

He runs towards me again, and I use the sword to cut the back of his legs, making him fall. He turns his head and looks up at me as I hit him with the sack, knocking him out. As I drag him through the arches, he moans softly. Once back at the building, I bang on the door until finally a demon opens the door.

"Nightmare? Are you here for your eleventh level?" The demon snarls at me, his eyes filled with joy at the prospect.

"No, but Daniel is!" I reply, looking down at my unconscious companion.

"An angel? Who told you to bring him here?" The demon asks, confused.

"The Masters did. I've also killed Jesus and Gabriel."

"Huh! There are no records of him coming here," the demon responds, looking at his board.

"That's because they are busy with my latest gifts. Four young girls."

"Ahh! That makes sense. I'll start working on this one then, and I'll let them be for a day before bringing it to their attention," the demon answers, grabbing Daniel by the leg and throwing him inside the building.

"Yes, you wouldn't want them to get angry. I better bring them the heads I promised I would," I reply.

"See you soon, Nightmare!" The demon laughs as he closes the door.

"Okay… I don't think so," I reply, after he's out of earshot, as I walk towards my freedom.

Liar

I've thrown up multiple times as we sit, here waiting for this angel to go away, but he just continues to mock all of the humans. The elevator door opens once again and standing there is Nightmare. He comes walking by with a blooded sack and stops dead in his tracks upon seeing Debbie.

"What the hell are you doing here, Debbie? I thought I told you to run to the west," he addresses her.

"Nightmare!" The angel yells. "Leave my soon-to- be victims alone! What brings you back this time? Is it time for me to show you how death works in the real world?"

"I'm sorry, were you talking to me, Michael? I couldn't hear what you were saying with all that crap coming out of your mouth again."

"Did you finally bring me a gift for having to put up with you coming through here all the time?" Michael continues, glaring at Nightmare.

Nightmare laughs and states.

"The only present I have or am ever going to bring you is pain, Michael. I've done something that none of you have done a day in your life. I killed the savior himself. His head is in this bag with Gabriel's."

"You didn't. I'm going to take that up to God and Lucifer. I'll finally have something to gloat over." Michael shouts.

"No, you won't. Face it, you are nothing more than a scavenger. Look at what you're doing to those people. All you do is maim and kill people."

"That's my job, Nightmare. I kill these people for them, and I'll kill you too," Michael answers.

Nightmare stands there laughing as he dangles the blooded sack in front of him. "You couldn't kill me on your best day, but you're still welcome to try."

"Oh, I will. And when I do, I'll be adored by many."

"I that a threat or a promise, Michael? I would hate for you to stick your feet in your mouth once again."

"Keep pushing me, Nightmare. I will bring you more pain than you have ever endured in your life."

"I guess that was a threat. I knew you were scared of me. I knew it from the first day I saw you. You have no guts unless they're chained to a wall."

"You're asking for a beating now, Nightmare. Get ready to die."

"I'm asking for nothing. You're the one that thinks you're so big and tough. I'm willing to teach you that you're nothing more than a mouth."

I watch as the two run towards each other, and begin fighting. Nightmare pushes Michael further away from us, against the wall, but just as we get ready to make a run for it, another angel comes from the stairs and runs towards Michael.

"Stop this right now!" He shouts. "Do you know what will happen to you, Michael? If God comes down here and sees you doing this, you'll get thrown into the pits. Why did you let him goad you into this?"

"He says he has Jesus' head in the bag," Michael responds. "I told him to give it to me, and he wouldn't."

"Is Michael telling the truth, Nightmare? Did you kill Jesus?"

"Yes, I did. I slaughtered that fool so fast he didn't know what hit him. Then I killed Gabriel. I cut both their heads off, and now I'm off to receive my reward for killing them. Go now, Peril."

"What do you mean go?" Peril answers. "Are you going senile, Nightmare? That made no sense what's so ever. You're going to give over that bag to me, and I'll hand it to God."

Nightmare shouts even louder.

"That made sense to me. It means wherever I want to I can go away from you, Peril. I am not handing anything over to you or this piece of crap Michael. You want something, go earn it yourself. Just because you couldn't beat him doesn't mean you're going to enjoy the spoils of my victory."

We finally catch on to what Nightmare is trying to say, and head towards the stairs. Looking back at Nightmare, Michael and the other angel, Peril, are still distracted. We start making our way up the stairs, trying to make as little noise as possible, until finally we're out of view. We get to the top of the stairs and see a set of massive doors in

166

front of us. We put our ears up against the door, trying to hear anything, and listen to what sounds like taunting, but we can't make out what they are saying.

"What are they saying, Amanda?" David asks.

"I don't know, David. It's too quiet to understand." I reply. I don't tell him that it sounds like a child crying.

"Should we go in?"

"I don't know. I'm trying to figure out how many people are in there," I respond.

After a few minutes of waiting, Nightmare walks up the stairs glaring at us all.

"What the hell are you doing here, Debbie?" He whispers. "I told you to go to the west. You would have been safe. I don't know who the rest of you are but coming here was the worst decision you could make."

"My name's Amanda Jay. I was looking for the children when I came through the hole in the shower. I am still looking for those children right now," I answer, watching the look on his face change.

"I'm using those children right now. I just killed Jesus and Gabriel, I'm doing this in exchange for some power. You should've gone to the elevator, not the stairs when I said to go. I didn't mean come upstairs. You do realize you won't get out of here now, right? Now you are going to have to meet your makers. Peril's at the bottom of the stairs again, and he sure as hell isn't going to let you through. Once I go through these doors, you are going to be coming with me. Debbie, there was a reason I told you to go to the west; these are the last people from Purgatory. They could have eventually figured out a way to bring Purgatory back. I thought you could help them with that. And you Amanda, you do realize, you are not going back to the living again?"

"I realize that now. I am just tired of running away from Jesus, and everyone else in this abandoned place. I want to make a stand," I reply.

"I know running gets tiresome, but what you should've thought about how these men have survived a multitude of attacks from Heaven and Hell, and they're still alive to tell the tale. They would've been your best choice to defeat God and Lucifer. Now you've doomed them all. There's no place left to go but through these doors."

"I'm sorry. Nobody ever explained the rules of this place to me, but I want to know where the children are," I respond, looking at the anger in his eyes.

"The children are safe, beyond this door. The girls are in a fire cage right now. I was using them to get power, so I could close all these doors for good. I don't know how this is going to work with me bringing you in here now, though."

"Why would you do that Nightmare? Why would you sacrifice children, for power, even if you have good intentions?" I ask, my eyes filling with tears.

"These are the first set of children I've brought them in decades. These kids are my ticket to close all the unholy thirteens. Once I do that, they will die. People will be staying in their bodies from this day forward. No one will go to Heaven, no one will go to Hell, and people will go to Purgatory once more. Eventually this world will die, and God and Lucifer's partnership will dissolve with no one coming in. Four children are worth the price of that happening."

"No child is worth that price," I whisper, angry he would even suggest that.

"You'll see. People will no longer die because they are in the wrong place, at the wrong time. People would die according to their fate. Another decade and the deaths are going to be sharply increasing; you'll have hundreds, even thousands, of people every day that will die. It won't be natural, and soon your world would fill with sand as this world has. All the sand here used to be people. When you come through these portals, your body instantaneously turns to sand. There's no returning to the living once you are here. So, to answer your question again, four children are worth it."

"There must be some way to stop them other than using children," I reply, confused by why he is arguing this.

"No there isn't. For years, people have tried killing God and Lucifer to no benefit. They have no power here, and with no power, you can't fight someone with power. That's why, they had to destroy Purgatory. Purgatory could equalize the forces. That's why they took Jesus' power away. Jesus was trying to kill everyone over there, in hopes of cutting off people going through the arches. Now I killed Jesus because I wanted too. I killed more than I should have; I was only supposed to kill one of Jesus' guards, but I killed Jesus to ensure the people of the wastelands wouldn't have to run anymore."

"I am sorry, Nightmare..." I state, as what he is saying is making more sense.

"As I told you, Debbie, I'm already on my tenth level because I was defiant. I learned from each mistake I made, and every person I trusted. God and Lucifer will not come out of this place; they won't send their forces into the wastelands. Individuals who survive in the Badlands would be free of this tyranny. There aren't many people alive in the Badlands. I needed permission to go after Jesus because he was still the son of God. We're going to have to go in here and say you are my prisoners, so don't say anything. Let me do all the talking; you have already screwed up my plan enough."

"I don't want to go in there. I'll stay right here," Debbie replies.

"Debbie, you are going to go in there even if I have to throw you through those doors face first. Now, remember, nobody says anything to God or Lucifer. If you do, you're on your own. Do you understand?"

"I understand. I don't like it, but I understand." I reply, a deep sadness overwhelming me.

"Good. Whatever you do, do not look at them directly either. Anything you can say will just irritate them. Just look at the floor and kneel down."

"Fine," Debbie mutters angrily.

"You. Amanda. I know you care about those kids, and on any other day I would have left them alone, but this is a once in a lifetime chance to close that door. If not now, it would never be closed."

The curse of 13

Looking at him, I can't tell if he's being sincere or not. "I don't feel it's right, and if those children get hurt I'll come after you with everything I have!" I whisper.

"That's a fiery response, but if you don't stay quiet, you won't have to worry about doing anything."

"I'll stay quiet," I respond.

"You remind me of someone close to my heart Amanda. She meant a lot to me, and that is why you are still alive. Don't fight or I will be forced to do something I don't want to do. Understand?"

"Yes," I reply, narrowing my eyes as I look at him closely.

Face to face with evil

After making sure everyone is going to stay quiet, they all stand, and I push open the doors to see the four children in a cage surrounded by fire. God and Lucifer walk around the cage like sharks circling their prey.

"What do we have here, Nightmare? More gifts for us?" Lucifer asks, smiling.

"Of course, they're for us, Lucifer. There's no other reason for humans to be here?" God answers.

"I caught them on the stairs. Seems Michael and Peril aren't doing their jobs like you said they were," I reply, sternly.

"What the hell did you say?" Lucifer asks.

"You heard what I said, Lucifer. I caught them just outside the door. This door."

"You're a liar. Nightmare," God shouts.

"If I'm a liar, why are they here with me and not downstairs with Michael?" I state, looking at Lucifer nod his head in agreement.

"You know he's right, God. There's no way they'd be here if they didn't get by Michael and Peril."

"Get Michael and Peril in here now!" God shouts.

The curse of 13

"I'll get them for you, but nobody touches these humans until I get back. Give me your word," I reply, watching as the anger on their faces grow.

"Yes, Nightmare. You have my word." Lucifer says, resentfully.

I go back through the doors and yell, "Peril! Michael! You're wanted upstairs. Now!"

The door swings open shortly after, and in walks Michael and Peril.

"What the hell's going on Michael? Peril? How the hell did these humans get here?" God shouts at them.

"I don't know my Lord? I know Nightmare picked a fight with us," Michael answers, looking worried.

"I picked it with you? You always pick it with me, Michael. You always want to be the one to bring God and Lucifer my gifts," I reply, arrogantly.

"I do not. I do what I'm told to do, and that's all I do."

"And as I always say, Michael, you have crap coming out of your mouth," I reply.

"For some reason… I believe Nightmare has a point," Lucifer adds. "How else would they get past you if you were doing your job as you say you were?"

"Of course you would believe, Nightmare. After all, Nightmare's your creation, is he not?" Michael blurts out.

"Yes, he is, but I believe him because what he says is true. Why would Nightmare tell us lies when he has so much at stake?"

"I have to ask myself why would Michael lie?" God interrupts.

"Michael would because you would send him to the pit. There is no way Nightmare could've gotten these people through that whole floor himself," Lucifer argues.

"God. I swear I would not do anything like that. I swear it," Michael begs, dropping to his knees.

"Why then did you want to bring up my bag and show God? You even know which heads I have in this bag," I state.

"Which heads are in the bag, Michael? Tell me the truth," God says.

"Jesus and Gabriel," He answers, his mouth quivering.

"Jesus' head is in the bag? You were supposed to go after Gabriel or one of the other ones guarding him," God shouts, his eyes wide.

"I went for them too, but Jesus was closest so I took a swing at him and then Gabriel. I fulfilled my end of the deal," I reply, watching God's eyes burn through my soul.

"Yes, Nightmare. You went far and above what we asked of you," Lucifer answers. "You've also gifted us more people."

"You failed, Nightmare. You will suffer the thirteenth level for this," God yells.

"How did he fail, God? He performed more than initially expected of him," Lucifer argues.

"He failed because he killed my son. That was not part of the bargain."

The curse of 13

"What do you mean? He did say he was going to kill them all. Don't tell me you're going soft, God. Truthfully it was a blameless death."

"Yes, you did say that didn't you, Nightmare. Well, you have gained your little power in exchange for these children. Now, what do you expect for these adults?"

"I think for the three Purgatory boys here, I'd like to watch Michael and Peril fight it out to the death," I exclaim, looking at them both, curling the corner of my mouth just enough for them to know I'm smiling.

"Are you kidding me, God?" Michael protests. "You cannot allow this abomination to dictate our fates."

"I am not kidding. Michael has been a pain in my side for so long already. You do nothing when I bring it to your attention, and they are always harassing me. You say they're doing their job, but they let people through. I think you have it in for me, God," I reply, intensifying my stare.

"I have nothing in for you, boy. You are a whiny, sniveling, little monster. Every time you have something new to bring us, you always find a way to get your way. I am tired of that."

"Hold up. Have you been interfering with Nightmare?" Lucifer interrupts.

"I have not been messing with your creation, Lucifer. He's a liar," God insists.

"Nightmare, what has happened when you cross Michael and Peril's path?" Lucifer continues.

"Michael is always trying to take the ones I bring to you from me. Peril does the same. They are always threatening to kick my backside even though I've kicked their backsides every time. I have proven my worth to both of you. Even in the darkest of times, I've been there for you." I reply, looking directly at them both.

"Yes, you have been, Nightmare. I do believe Nightmare has made a point, and my demons should be on the floor below us."

"That's not part of our deal, Lucifer," God shouts angrily.

"And it's not part of our agreement that your Angels interrupt my messenger either."

"Even if they did mess with him a little bit, that doesn't make up for rearranging our agreement."

"Our arrangement was unmistakable. You and your Angels were not to mess with my messenger, and apparently you have been messing with my messenger."

"Okay, fine. Michael and Peril will do battle until one of them is dead. We will stick to the original agreement, and my Angels will no longer interfere with your messenger. Deal?"

"Yes. If I hear from Nightmare one more time that your Angels have interfered with him bringing us souls, I'll deal with it myself. Now that we've dealt with that, what do you want for those two young women Nightmare?"

"And keep it reasonable, Nightmare," God adds.

"I would also like my territory increased. I don't want to just deal with just one little place anymore. I want to address the world. I want to be able to make doors and make thirteen the curse word of everyone living. I want to be able to pick off people every second of every day."

"That is a tough bill to fill, Nightmare. Do you understand what that would mean?" Lucifer answers.

"Lucifer does have a point. Do you think you can handle the whole world?" God adds.

"Yes, I could handle that well. I'd bring so many people at a time, and I wouldn't have to stop until the last person was drained from the living world. With the power you give me, and if you increase my territory to the world, I wouldn't have to stop. I could drain the living world in several years. That's what I want in exchange for these two women."

"I must talk with Lucifer before deciding this matter," God replies.

Lucifer and God walk back to their own thrones and lean in behind the fire again. Their voices are louder, and I can tell they're arguing.

"What are you doing Nightmare?" Amanda whispers.

"Shut up, Amanda. Do not say another word to me. Just stay down there."

"Great going, Nightmare. You're nothing more than a little baby snitch," Michael says, walking over to me.

"You're the one that's placed yourself in this mess, Michael. I told you to leave me alone while I was conducting my business." I respond.

"How did you get those people by us?" Peril asks.

"I didn't, Peril. You and Michael were the ones watching. All I did was bring Jesus and Gabriel's heads. They were already at the top of the stairs when I got here. Anything else that happens is on you two," I reply, watching him try to figure it out.

"You better hope God overturns Peril and I fighting to the death. Otherwise Peril or I will be on you so bad you'll wish you were dead."

"Why would they overturn that decision? These are the last three people from Purgatory. Do you know what that means? I know you know the answer," I reply, looking at the fear in their eyes.

"I know what it means. They'll now run the other side," Michael responds.

"Good job, Michael. Too bad your God didn't trust in you enough to let you go hunting." I respond, snidely.

"God wanted us here protecting him from Lucifer."

"So, what you're saying, is God didn't trust you enough to leave his side, while I'm allowed everywhere."

"Enough chatting down there!" God's voice booms. "Michael. Peril. Front and center. You may pick your weapons."

"Yes, my Lord. I'll pull this sword of ages."

"Peril, what weapon do you pick?"

"I'll pick the spear of destiny."

"Peril, you're allowed to have last words and you can address anyone in this room."

"I would like to say it has been an honor and a pleasure serving you, my Lord. I have always stood by your side, in good times and bad. I am sorry if my actions dictated differently towards Nightmare. I am sorry Lucifer; I meant nothing by impeding on Nightmare's duties. Michael, may we have a great fight and I hope the better of us wins."

"Thank you," Michael repsonds. "I also hope the better man wins. It has been an honor to serve you, my Lord. Lucifer; it has been an honor to serve under you as well. How these five people got by me, I will never know. I know I fulfilled my duty, and I can only hope that one day you may forgive me for it. I have no excuse, and I accept any punishments due to me. I also wish to apologize to Nightmare. I know we've never seen eye to eye on anything, but I can only hope you will forgive me down the road."

"I do have something to say also, my Master. I'd ask that the children be released from the fire cell. I will watch them as the fight goes on. This way they have the room to fight," I interject, looking at the frightened look on their young faces.

"Good point, Nightmare. You'll watch all nine of them until the fight's finished, and then you'll bring them up one at a time, so we can inspect our prizes. Is this acceptable to you?" Lucifer responds.

"I shall start with the oldest and work to the youngest, thus ensuring you get the best quality at the end," I reply, confidently.

"You always love giving us the best at the last moment. I accept. What about you, God?"

"I'll agree with Lucifer. You may bring them to us oldest to youngest; the duel will begin once the children are with Nightmare."

"Before I forget, Nightmare, here is your power as promised. This will help you watch them better."

"Thank you, I will not let you down." I say as a blue flash of light hits my hand. The flames disappear from the cage and the children run over to me. They sit down at my feet, and I can see they want to say something but are afraid. Looking at them, I give them a tiny nod, and that seems to ease them a bit.

"Begin!"

Peril and Michael walk around each other, counter-clockwise, trying to get a feel for the other's strengths and weaknesses. Peril thrusts the spear forward in an attempt to intimidate Michael, but Michael wields the sword like an expert, turning and twisting it to show Peril he's covered on all sides. They continue this excellent dance for at least half an hour.

"What do you call this?" Lucifer finally interjects. "I've seen the tortured fight better than this. I want to see hurting on an epic scale."

While God and Lucifer's focus is on Michael and Peril, I take a moment to talk to the children.

"You okay?" I ask, smiling at them.

"Yes, Peter, but why do they keep calling you Nightmare?"

"They call me Nightmare because of the nightmarish stuff I do to others. I promised you children I'd not let you be harmed. Do you still trust me?" I ask.

"I am trying Peter," Emma replies, her eyes filled with tears. "There's just so much going on. I don't know what to trust or believe anymore?"

"Don't worry, Emma. I promised on my heart that I would not let anything happen to you. You need to think of that."

"I will try hard, to understand that Peter."

I lean over to David and whisper in his ear. He jerks back after he hears what I say and shakes his head. I lean over and whisper in his ear again, this time patting Emma's face softly. He finally nods yes. We go back to watching the resulting fight between Michael and Peril. After about another hour of fighting, Michael and Peril are still untouched.

"I call this a draw," God bellows.

"To hell with that idea, God," Lucifer screams. "As they seem not have something to fight for, I'll add an amendment to this match. Since they're fighting is going nowhere."

"They fought right, Lucifer. There is no need to add anything to this match."

"Let's make this interesting, God. They'll fight five demons each. The match will be over when one of them dies."

"If they survive all five demons, then what?" God asks.

"If they survive all five demons, then we will place them on the level above the pits. They will live there."

"There won't be any other addenda, Lucifer?" God asks, grimacing.

Lucifer shakes his head and responds.

"No, there'll be no more changes."

"Okay, five demons each."

We stand there and wait as the doors swing open and massive beasts with teeth and claws come walking in, followed by another and another until ten demons are standing in the room.

"God? Lucifer? May I take the prisoners just outside, so they aren't harmed in any way during this match up?" I shout, abruptly.

"Good idea Nightmare. Just outside the room," Lucifer responds.

"Come on all of you, let's go," I shout, as everyone gets up. We walk outside the room and all sit down together. Once the doors closed, they began chattering among one another.

"Whatever you are thinking, don't believe it. You won't like the result," I state, glaring at the adults.

"Why are you doing this to us Nightmare?" Ray asks. "You let Debbie go. You didn't bring her here, why?"

"Yes, I let Debbie go, but she came back here. Had she kept going west, she would have never seen me again," I whisper, annoyed.

"I'm sorry Nightmare. I thought if we made a stand we could end this," Amanda says.

"Five people. Five people aren't going to stop what's happening here. Armies are what prevents this from happening. What you might have succeeded in doing is creating a little interruption. One person can make a great hero, but there's also common sense that should tell you when the odds aren't in your favor."

"We thought if we stood up, we'd have at least a little chance to make a better world here."

"You can't do it that way. Have you been to the wastelands lately? You see the carnage out there? The sands of billions of people flowing with no end in sight? You can't stop a machine from eating everything in eye view. A machine has no heart, and it feels no conscience. The only way to stop a machine is to take it apart, piece by piece, until it no longer works. Unfortunately for you, common sense has come too late. You don't think I want peace and joy, but I do want that more than anything. I was there in Purgatory when the attack happened. I watched a million people turn to sand within years. I watched the people I loved turned to grit. Faces I can no longer remember are lost in eternity. I've spent years just trying to remember an image that remotely looks like my mother, or my father, or even a friend. I can't remember, anything about what they look like, so yes I made a deal to become what I am. You can call me a monster, you can call me a murderer, but I do what I have to do to survive here among angels and demons. I wish you had stayed in the wastelands. This brings me no joy at all, and I will use what I have to to get what I want," I exclaim, memories flooding back, as I try to keep myself composed.

"I would think you would want freedom? That's what everyone yearns to have," Amanda responds.

"Yes, freedom is what I want, but freedom comes with a hefty price on my end. I have nothing... everyone I know is gone. Do you know the reason I am not dead right now? I'm not dead right now because of a demon that took me to Lucifer. I was a lapdog. I did some of the worst jobs just to stay alive. I was even there when they signed that final agreement after Purgatory fell. Who do you think was the third party that signed? That's me. I heard every single agreement between them, including the one to destroy all living humans and assimilate them into one power. Both Heaven's laws and Hell's laws bind me. Thirteen rules I have no choice but to obey," I state, remembering every little piece of those agreements.

"I'm sorry, Nightmare. If I could take back anything I've done, I would take back coming here. I can't take it back, but you could help us escape this."

"You're the one they call Amanda, right?" I ask, looking at her face closer.

"Yes, people call me Amanda."

"Well Amanda, have you ever broken your arm and had to lift something heavy with no cast or anything protective?" I reply, annoyed.

"No, why would you ask that?"

"The first time you disobey, that is your punishment. Four weeks of walking around with boulders attached to broken arms. The pain is great and agonizing. Imagine what level eleven would be for me. Imagine yourself disemboweled as they strip every little piece of you apart. There isn't a moment's peace for six months. You never forgot the pain, and you'll do anything you have to not feel that pain or worse again," I reply as I shudder at the thought of that.

"Aren't there any possible ways out of here?"

"That'll be between you, God, and Lucifer. I cannot do anything but make sure that after the fight, I take each one of you to them. I hope you can forgive me some time," I state, looking sternly at Amanda.

"Peter. You said we could trust you," Emma whispers.

"You can, Emma. My word to you is as solid as gold," I reply, looking at her and smiling.

"You're telling lies to the children," Debbie shouts.

"Shut up, Debbie! I'm not telling lies to the children. While these four girls are with me, they'll be fine," I reply.

"You told me, once you are here that's it…"

"Yes, I said that and I mean it, but if you say one more word right now, I will watch you bleed. Do you understand what I am saying?" I state.

The noise gets louder behind the door, and everyone focuses on what may be happening in there.

"Nightmare, can I talk to you over there?" Amanda leans in and whispers, pointing to the other side of the door.

"Come on, make it quick," I reply, following her.

"I just want to know for my own personal piece of mind, do you really have the children's interest at heart? Or are you really truthful about sacrificing four children for the greater good?"

Leaning towards Amanda's ear, I whisper, "My plan was flawless before you lot showed up. I had worked on this for fifty years already, and now I cannot answer either question with any certainty. I hope by the end of this I will be able to answer you, but now I can't."

"You already have."

Anyone is helpful at this point.

As fellow officers scrap at anything possible to link these children disappearing to anything, the chatter soon turns to sorrow. I see the housekeeping woman walking towards me. "Hello, Edna, what can I do for you?"

"I found someone who might be able to help with that room, officer."

"Okay, we are willing to accept help from anyone at this point. Who are they?" I ask.

"Her name is Anna Smyth. She deals a lot with spirits. She'll be able to figure out what's going on here."

"Are you sure, Edna? We have exhausted all other leads to where these children went. The the last I'd want to do is waste a bunch of time on someone who isn't honest."

"She is, officer. She'll be here any minute, I promise."

"Okay, Edna. We'll talk to her and see what she has to say."

Walking away from Edna, I head back to room 14, and open the door slowly, trying to figure out where these children went. I find it hard to accept that four children disappeared without a trace. After about twenty minutes, Edna comes back with her friend. Edna stands next to a woman who looks like she might be in her thirties. She smiles and holds out her hand.

"Hello, Officer, my name is Anna Smyth."

"Good to meet you, Mrs. Smyth," I reply, shaking her hand. "Edna tells me you're an expert in this field?"

"Yes, I have a long history of dealing with spirits. Especially ones that tend not to be at rest."

"If that's the case, Mrs. Smyth, we have a real wingding here. This is also an active crime scene, so all I ask is that you touch as little as possible, please."

"I understand, officer. I shouldn't need to feel anything except for what may have been the last thing the children felt."

"That would be the shower. I hope you do not have to touch too many things in there, that's where the crime scene is."

"I'll try to move as little as possible. I just need to feel where they were last."

"Okay, good. Let's go into the room here and I'll show you."

"I already feel something stepping into this room. I feel like my head is crushed between two walls. This spirit is vicious. Please, let's go to the bathroom then. The atmosphere is different. Oh god, the spirits are even angrier in here. Were the children the last ones taken?"

"No, there were two officers, a forensic scientist, and a manager," I answer as I read from my notepad.

"I see. I can feel the portal right at the back of the shower. The sand on the shower floor symbolizes something passing. It's the transferring between body and soul."

"What are you trying to say? The sand is their bodies?" I ask, almost dumbfounded by what she is saying.

"In a matter of speaking, yes. You see, the spirit or soul keeps the body whole. Once that is removed, the body returns to the earth. This doesn't happen with people who die and then their soul leaves. The sand occurs when it is ripped from its body."

"I have a hard time believing that, but seeing as we don't have any other tangible evidence, I will believe every word you say," I reply, trying not to mock her.

"Thank you, officer. I know it must be hard to consider there is another side, but everything in the world has two sides. People have two sides; and life and death are the same with two sides. The thing that puzzles me about this, is these people were assimilated immediately. The color of the sand would suggest a transfer of the soul directly. Is there anyway we can test what is happening to these people?"

"I'm not sure what you mean, Mrs. Smyth?" I ask, confused by her question.

"I'm suggesting we find a person and test the theory of what's happening here with cameras recording."

"I don't think I can sanction that. If you want to see if someone's willing to do it, as long as they know the risks and are of sound mind, then I can't legally say no," I answer.

"Okay. I just want to see what is exactly happening. That would at least give us a clearer picture of how these people are turning to sand immediately."

"I can't tell you what happened either. When the two officers went missing…we have no idea what happened, except for the sand on the shower floor," I answer, saddened by thoughts of what their families will do now.

Perry Pankratz

You're going to pay for this.

A voice yells for us to come back in, so we stand and walk into a bizarre sight. Michael is on the floor, shredded into pieces, and the eight remaining demons are dragging Peril.

"I see you honored your side of the bargain, Nightmare," Lucifer states, staring at the bloody sight.

"Maybe I was wrong about you, Nightmare," God adds. "Everything I have seen today from you shows you are willing to do anything to be recognized as loyal."

"Thank you, Master. I have always tried to be loyal." I state, confidently.

"I knew from the moment I slaughtered everyone you knew, that I had picked the right one. You didn't cry or whine about them being dead, you just sat in Purgatory until we were ready. You are the most decent human I have ever met," Lucifer continues.

"Thank you, Master," I reply, smiling a little bit now.

"God and I have bequeathed you the honor of the world. From now on, you are free to open or create any door you want. Anything that makes thirteen is yours to rule now, unopposed. Your abilities to bring the living here with your drive and aptitude for cunningness are a prize for us all."

"I shall not let you down. You will see the change in people," I respond, happily.

"I know we will, Nightmare. Now, let's begin. Nring me that one standing right there."

"Ready for this Frank?" I ask, looking at the fear in his face.

"No, I am not…"

"Sorry, I have to do this. Let's go!" I pull on him as we walk up to their thrones, Frank looks at me, as if he's going to be sick, but I escort him all the way up to God, and then to Lucifer.

I proceeded back to the others, and with a great thunderous roar, Lucifer strikes him down dead. Everyone watches in horror as the man implodes. The children scream, and I walk over to them and kneel down.

"It's going to be alright… these people are making sure you have time to get ready, okay?" I whisper.

"Okay, Peter… I don't want that to happen to me, or my sisters," Denise answers.

"Don't worry, Denise. Nothing is going to happen to you. Any of you," I answer, smiling a little.

"That was one man from Purgatory. He is now with his brothers and sisters. Tell me, who are you two men and are you from Purgatory as well?" Lucifer asks, pointing to David.

"I refuse to answer you!" David shouts.

"Well, I think I will save you until after if you want to be defiant. You can watch your brother die before your eyes. Who are you then?" Lucifer asks, turning his attention to Ray.

"I am Ray."

"Well, Ray. You'll become assimilated as well. You see, you are the last one from Purgatory. Once you are absorbed, we will be able to end the wastelands. Will you be the next to stand before us?"

"No, Master. This is David and he will be the next to approach," I intervene.

We walk up to the throne, and this time I stop, letting, David go to the throne by himself as I walk back to the others. I kneel in front of the children who are afraid and try to reassure them.

"You promised nothing would happen to us," Emma whimpers.

"Yes, Emma, I did promise you nothing would happen to any of you, and I am true to my word. This is what I want you to do: when Lucifer begins to yell at God, you remember those rocks I gave you?" I ask.

"Yes? I still have mine. I think everyone else has there's, too," Emma replies as the other girls nod in agreement.

"Those are special rocks. You remember how I said those enabled you to come with me? Those will also take you home. You each have a different color rock. I want you to put them together and keep holding onto them. They will make a heart shape when put together, and you each hang on to your own piece. Once you put them together, within minutes you'll be back home in the room I got you from. Do this after Lucifer gets up and starts yelling at God. Do not do it a second before, ttherwise they will stop you from going home. Do you understand me, Emma?" I ask, smiling at all the children.

"Yes, Peter. I understand."

"Good. Thank you for all your help girls. I will never forget any of you for all your help." I respond, tears coming to my eyes as I look at their faces.

"We won't forget you either Peter," Emma replies.

"You can call me Nightmare. That's my real name, Emma." I answer, feeling saddened by their leaving.

"Can we give you a hug?"

"No, I don't want them to see. How about a finger touch?" I say, reaching out to touch each one of their fingers, as they begin to smile for the first time in a while. The moment is ruined by Lucifer's yelling.

"What? You promised David if he killed me he'd be sitting in my spot? That's the last straw. You're going to pay, God."

"Lucifer have you gone crazy? I didn't say anything? What the hell is wrong with you?"

"Liar. First Nightmare and your angel's meddling, and now these blatant lies! You have broken this agreement, and you underhandedly attempted to have me killed!"

"I haven't lied. You're the one violating the contract with these outrageous accusations."

As both God and Lucifer walk down hurriedly from their thrones, I watch as they stare each other down. Each one turns into fire and lightning, and like a tornado they soon disappear behind it. As they begin to fight and yell within the storm, I look at the girls.

"Now, Denise, Emma, Amy, and Carol!" I whisper. I watch as the girls begin, placing their stones in the shape of a heart on the floor.

"Make sure it looks like a heart!" I remind them.

"What are you doing Nightmare?" Debbie asks, seeing us.

"Keeping my promise," I reply.

"A promise? You never made a promise to me?"

"I promised these children they were going home, So I'm going to send them back."

"How can you send them back when you couldn't send me back?" Debbie asks, furious.

"I can't send you back. Each of those stones is part of my heart; I promised I would send them back, and they have more than earned their way back... they followed everything I said. The best gift I can give them is to send them home to be with their families." I reply.

"What about my family, Nightmare? You stole me from them."

"Don't even go there, Debbie. You are old enough. Just because I said I was your grandpa to get you in here doesn't mean I owe you crap. You came to this place of your own free will," I answer, sternly.

"Debbie. I would rather see the children go home too," Amanda intervenes. "Just let the kids go back to their families, at least you'll be here with Brad. You won't be alone."

"That's not fair, Amanda. I should be living still. His lies are why I'm here, and I should be living in my dream home."

"Just let it go. You'll have Brad. I'll gladly stay here if those children can go home. This is no place for a child. You know that yourself."

"There's nothing I can do about it, Debbie. I gave each one of these four young women a piece of my heart knowing that I would be getting power in exchange for them. Once I had that, I could power my heart to bring these children to the last place they were. Once they are safely through, I am going to close every single thirteen doorways to this place. No one will ever have to suffer again at the hands of these two," I explain, looking towards God and Lucifer.

"You didn't have to take us either! You tricked me to follow you. You are going to take me back!"

"Yes, I coaxed you here, but I owe you nothing, Debbie. I did what I had too. You were in the right room at the wrong time. I'm sorry Debbie, there are only four stones, one for each of the children that make up my entire heart. There isn't a grain of heart left for anyone else," I reply, frustrated by Debbie's ignorance towards a happy reunion of child and parents.

"That's not right. I want to live too!"

"Come on, Debbie," Amanda yells, angered. "These kids deserve to live the rest of their life with their parents. He could have helped you, yes, but he's helping these four young girls. He told you to go to the west, and it is my fault we are here. I'll accept whatever comes from my decision, but let the children go home…"

Before anyone can do anything to stop it, Debbie pulls away from Amanda and grabs the pink stone, pushing Carol aside, and places it to complete the heart symbol. A glow engulfs the three children and Debbie, and in a flash they all disappear from the room.

"That cruel piece of garbage!"

My Babies

Looking around the bathroom, I remove the unnecessary tools and forensic equipment making room for Anna, who has a plan to try to open a door of some sort to the other side. After watching the last extra lights being carried out, I allow Anna through, and she brings in her book along with a couple of candles. Anna places the candles on each side of the shower door and looks at me as she opens a book.

"I don't know if this is going to work, officer, but according to this book, this should open a doorway to the other side, so we should be able to see what is going on."

Even before she can start speaking the words to open the door, the wall of the shower begins to ripple like water, creating a distorted mosaic. We hear what sounds like a thunderstorm in the shower, and little streaks of blue light form in the center that are growing outward.

"What's going on, Anna?" I ask, stunned.

"Do you see what's happening?" Anna shouts.

"I see it, but I do not believe it. What's going on?"

"I am not exactly sure. I haven't started saying anything, so nothing should be happening"

The ripples begin to stretch out along with the blue streaks of light and open up like a black hole. Soon a flash of light explodes from the center, blinding us all. As we cover our eyes trying to regain sight, a child's voice becomes clearer.

"Who are you?" I ask, still trying to regain a view of something more than light and shadows.

"My name is Denise, where's mom?" The child replies.

"You're one of those missing girl, aren't you?" I inquire, seeing her clearly now.

There's another flash, and a second child appears.

"Denise, where's mom?" She asks.

"Don't worry, Amy. I am sure we will see her soon."

"Yes, you both will see your mom shortly. Where are the other two?" I ask, looking at both of them stepping out of the shower.

Another flash, and a woman appears, screaming for everyone to get out of her way.

"Whoa! Quit pushing these children," I reply angrily as I stop her. "Sergeant, can you take this woman and hold her until we figure out what's going on?"

"Yes, come with me, Miss," The sergeant says, grabbing the woman's arm.

"No, let me go!"

"Calm down, Miss," I respond, as she walks by me.

There's yet again another flash of light, and another girl appears.

"Emma!"

"Denise! Amy! Where's Carol?" This new child asks.

"That woman stole Carol's stone to get back. She should be in jail!"

The curse of 13

"What's your name, Miss?" The Sergeant asks.

"Debbie Johnson," the woman answers.

"Denise? Can you tell me what you meant exactly when you said she stole your sister's stone? Get another officer here to keep an eye on this woman as well," I say to the sergeant. "Okay, can you tell me what's going on Denise?" I ask, calmly, watching as tears trickle down her face.

"Yes. There was a boy who took us from this room. His name was Peter or Nightmare. He gave us each a stone to hold. One for Amy, Carol, Emma, and myself. He told us he needed help killing an evil person who had his friend, so we went to help. When we got there, the bad men were God and Lucifer. While they started fighting, my sisters and I were told to put the colored stones into the shape of a heart, and that that would bring us back. That woman there, Debbie, she took Carol's stone from her and pushed her down, and Debbie came back here in her place. Our sister Carol is still in the wastelands of Heaven and Hell."

"Okay... let's see if I got this right. That woman, Debbie Johnson, stole a stone from your sister, Carol, and when you placed the stones in a heart shape it enabled you to come back here. Correct?" I ask, confused.

"Yes, that's why we're back."

"Do you still have these stones on you?" I ask, curiously.

"I don't think so. I wasn't holding anything when I came through here," she responds, looking around.

"Okay, Denise. I'm going to see what I can do about arresting Debbie for stealing," I respond, looking at Debbie with disgust.

"Where's mom and dad?" Denise asks.

"Don't worry about your parents. They will be down here shortly. They are in the lobby right now. You and your sisters just have a seat on the bed, and I'll be right back," I reply, smiling, knowing they will be together soon.

I walk towards Debbie to get her side of the story.

"Okay Debbie, Denise tells me you stole a stone from her sister, Carol. Is this true?" I ask, watching her erratic reactions.

"No, I didn't steal anything; I deserved to live as well, like everyone else," she responds, crossing her arms.

"What do you mean you deserve to live as well as everyone else? I asked if you stole anything. How'd you get back here Debbie?" I ask, angrily.

"I received a stone to place in a heart shape. That's how I'm back here."

"Who gave you this stone Debbie?" I ask.

"I'm not sure of their name?"

"You know something, I think I believe Denise. I believe that you stole their sister's stone to get back here."

"What if I did, officer? Are you going to put me in jail for a month or two for stealing a hunk of junk stone from a kid?"

"No, unfortunately, I can't charge you with that. I will say that makes you a horrible person, right up there, with the scum of the earth," I shout, angrily.

"Well, at least I'm alive. That's all that matters to me. I'm not answering any more of your questions, and I'm leaving."

"No, you don't have to answer any more of my questions, but you're not leaving either Debbie."

"You have no right to hold me here!"

"Yes, I do. You see, we're looking into the disappearance of people from this room," I state, sternly. "You can explain what happened to Carol to her mother, Karen when she gets in here." I state.

"No! That's your job to do. I have nothing to say to anyone."

"Yes, this is part of my job, but since you know exactly what happened to her daughter, I'll leave it up to you." I state, utterly disgusted by her selfishness.

A Hellfire burns

As God and the Devil continue their spirited fight, not long after Denise, Emma, and Amy disappeared, Carol begins crying, Amanda holds her close and tries to ease the child's tears. We watch as the building starts to tremble a little. Looking at Amanda and Carol, I make eye contact with Ray.

"Ray? We have to get out of here now."

"What? Oh, yes. Where's David?"

"I don't know? I can't see him." Amanda answers.

"He was probably killed just as the fight began. Let's get out of here now!" I exclaim, hurriedly, as Amanda and Carol run to the door. I open it and we all run down the spiral staircase. Stopping at the bottom, I see the look of fear on Carol's face.

"Look at me, Carol. Don't worry about what you are seeing. This is not real, okay? Once they're done the fighting, whoever wins is going to be pissed when they find us gone. Let's get to the elevator and get out of here," I shout, urgently.

We just start making our way to the elevators when the door opens, and Peril comes walking up to us.

"What're you doing back down here, Nightmare? Why are you taking this child, woman, and man? They belong to God and Lucifer now."

"They are a gift to me, for my service. They belong to me." I reply. Before Peril can say anything else, I raise my hand and use the power I was given to rip his heart out of his chest. He stands there momentarily and looks at me bewildered before he falls to his knees and then thuds down on the floor, dead. We continue to the elevator, and once the elevator opens up, Ray stops dead in his tracks. He looks at us and looks back at the moaning people chained to the wall.

"I am going to stay here and free these people from this wall. I would never forgive myself if I don't do something good while I am in the house of pain," Ray states.

"I can't promise you'll make it out of here," I answer, seeing the determination on his face. I push on the eye as he starts untying people as the door closes. The elevator shakes as the building rumbles a bit more than before. Once the door opens, Demons and Angels stand around, looking confused as we step out. A few growl and snarl, looking at us. Zozo comes walking to the front of the line sniffing.

"You! I smelled you before. What are you doing coming out of there?" He asks.

"I was told to take them to the other buildings!" I exclaim, sternly, looking him straight in the eyes.

"Why you of all people?" Zozo asks, suspiciously.

"I showed them my worth, so now I am trusted by them both!" I state, arrogantly. "Now move, I have to get them over to receive some pain."

"Well, you seem to have power…take them then!"

I can see Amanda's hand turning purple from Carol's grip. As we start making our way through the maze of Angels and Demons standing there, we're almost to the door before Zozo yells, "Nightmare, stop!"

We come to a stop and I look back As Zozo comes walking towards us. "What?" I ask, annoyed.

"What is going on upstairs anyway? They are shaking the building."

"Last I saw, they were torturing the others. They wanted to be left up there?" I explain, shrugging.

Zozo looks at me for a moment before shaking it off an returning to the group. We head out the sliding doors, and run like hell, not even turning back to see if anyone is behind us. After about a half hour, we finally make it to the arches which are beginning to light up a little. Running through the arches and into the sand dunes, we stop after another fifty feet, finally looking behind us.

"What happened to the winds, Nightmare? It's so calm and peaceful now." Amanda asks.

"Yes, isn't this great. The agreement between God and the Devil failed, so now they no longer hold the fate of Purgatory. With Jesus and his cronies dead on this side, everyone is free." I exclaim, smiling at Amanda.

The curse of 13

"Nightmare, I have to ask you something, and if you don't want to answer, that's fine, but…"

"I think I know what you want to ask, Amanda. You want to know why I did everything I did and acted like an asshole while doing it," I reply, looking straight into her eyes.

"Well, yeah."

I look towards the arches as they begin to glow an orange color. Ice forms, encrusting the arches, as the opening closes and seals everyone inside. Turning back towards Amanda, I answer, "I guess we have some time; it's going to be a long walk. Come here, Carol, let me help you up on my shoulders." I reply, picking her up, and onto my shoulders.

"What's going on with those aches, Nightmare?"

"Have you heard of the saying, until hell freezes over?" I ask.

"Yes, I have heard that, but I thought that was more to do with not doing something?"

"That is true, but what you're looking at is the official closing of Heaven and Hell. The demons and angels in those arches have utopia for eternity, Amanda." I exclaim, smiling as we walk. "I guess you wanted to know why I am who I am." I reply.

"Yes, if you don't mind telling me?"

"I don't mind… you remind me of the love of my life. She was my everything to me, and then Jesus killed her." I reply, as tears begin to form.

"Oh, I am so sorry."

"When I was sent to purgatory, after the Devil killed me, the waiting list for people moving on to Heaven and Hell was long, and I mean decades long. The Devil killed me because I was going to replace his last soul taker. Well, apparently God was waiting for the man sitting next to me, but as I said, it would be decades before we would move on," I explain.

"Can I ask why the wait was so long?"

"The wait time was so long because when someone dies, it takes a long time to realize you have died. All the time you spend here helps you come to realize you are no longer living. Once you are able to move on, you go where you go. Some come back to walk the earth, and others go to Heaven or Hell. Most times, it is a thirty to forty year wait, but it never seems that long."

"Oh my God! That is a long time to just sit there and wait."

"Yes, I know. I was sitting there when God and the Devil formed their union and attacked Purgatory. I saw the Angels and Demons burst through the doors. Everyone was scared, including me. They were swinging at anyone trying to escape, killing children, women, and men. After everyone was dead and the floor was red, a couple of Angels grabbed the man sitting next to me. Shortly after, the Devil grabbed me and he took me to Hell where he told me I was going to be his soul taker. I don't know how long went by before I was the third at the meeting between God and the Devil. They signed a pact, joining them together. They had already been working on their version of utopia, but once they signed, that very moment was when everything changed. They destroyed both Heaven and Hell in one swoop. Leaving what you witnessed- a damned place for all," I exclaim, fighting back the tears that want to come.

"Oh, I'm sorry Nightmare, that's awful. I wish there was something I could do to take back all the things I thought about you."

"Don't worry. I have been a lot worse in people's minds, I am sure," I reply, smiling a little more.

"I still like you Nightmare!" Carol speaks up.

"I like you too, Carol. How's the view up there?" I ask, trying to look up at her.

"Good, but where are we going?"

"Oh, that's a surprise. I still intend to keep my promise to you, Carol," I exclaim, smiling at her.

"Nightmare, did you have this planned all along?"

"No. While I was going through my tenth level pain I overheard Zozo the demon, and another angel talking about what would happen if the agreement between Lucifer and God was broken. So, as I was in severe pain, I started trying to think of a way to break this agreement between them. Thankfully, there were finally kids that came and stayed in that room. Four of them, to be exact. I started thinking that these four young girls could be the ticket. I know God and Lucifer both love kids in a bad way. I figured I'd give them each a piece of my heart to hold, knowing if I could get power in exchange for them that I could send them home as soon as I got the power. The near devastating part was leaving those young women with those monsters so I could go kill Jesus and Gabriel. Once I had enough tension built between God and the Devil, I knew one would flip. I was wondering if it was going to work after you all showed up. I hadn't taken the human cause into account, and once I thought about it for a bit, I realized I could get more. That's why I asked to control everything in the world. Knowing I could close access to Heaven and Hell, the world would be a better place once again. I am so sorry, Carol, that I had to use you to get what I wanted," I say, rubbing her arm.

"I'm not mad at you, Peter. You sent my sister's home to be with mom and dad. Maybe I can visit them one day."

"Don't worry, Carol. Soon you will be home. I promise you that," I exclaim, giving a smile to Amanda and Carol.

"What are you up to Nightmare?" Amanda asks.

"Nothing much, just thinking about what I would like to do to Debbie," I reply, smiling.

Coming home.

As I'm standing by the bathroom door, Amy walks towards me and asks, "Is mom coming?"

"Yes, she should be here in a moment," I reply, looking towards my sergeant for confirmation.

"Where's Carol?" I hear Karen shout.

"We're still trying to figure that one. Right now, just comfort the three children you have right now, and let us try to figure out the rest," I answer.

"Okay. Thank you, officer. Thank you from the bottom of my heart."

"You're welcome Mrs..." I start to say before being interrupted.

"I want out of here now!" Debbie shouts.

"You just wait there, Mrs. Johnson," I reply, watching Karen and her children walking out of the room. "Okay Mrs. Johnson, tell me one more time what happened here," I say, getting angrier by the second.

"I already told you what happened, officer. I want to go home now. You have no right to hold me here any longer."

"Listen, Mrs. Johnson. There's a child still missing, and I want to find this child, so you will help me. I don't care if your feelings hurt, or how big a piece of scum you feel like right now, you're going to help me," I state, disgusted by every word she says as she continues.

"Like I said, 'Nightmare' or whatever the hell he calls himself, coaxed me in here and then sent me to the dead."

"Okay, so what happened after that?"

"After I was trying to find my way back here, I ran into a couple people. One of them was the manager of the hotel. Amanda, I think...."

"You mean the manager Amanda Jay?" I ask, surprised.

"Yes. She was okay with staying over there as long as the children got to come home. I should've been here the whole time, so yes I figured I should be here."

"Yes, we've already determined you're a scum of the Earth person. I want to know..." I start to say.

The bathroom door slams shut, interrupting me. I turn around as quick as I can, but before I can get any words out, the lights begin flickering on and off, and dark blue light forms at the back of the shower. A face starts to emerge through the wall, yelling.

"You're a coward, Debbie! Stealing a little girl's hopes? You now belong to me. You're going to come with me and pay for what you did!"

"No!" Debbie screams "I'm not going back there. I'm going to live my life now."

"You have no choice. You stole Carol's chance to come back because of your greed. You'll live over here, and I am sending her back to where she belongs."

The curse of 13

She pushes me to the side, and runs for the bathroom door, trying to open it with all the strength she can muster. Officers on the other side of the door begin banging and yelling themselves, and I stand there wondering, *"Oh my God, am I going to be the next to go?"*

The spirit of a teenage boy comes out of the shower, looks at me and states, "don't worry, you are safe, but this piece of crap is coming back with me!"

"I won't stop you!" I reply, fearful of what he could do to me.

He grabs Debbie by the neck, and she screams for me to help her, but I stand there just watching, frozen with fear.

"Stop him! You're a police officer, shoot him."

"What the hell's going on? Let us in!" The officers on the other side of the door yell.

"You came back here because you stole Carol's stone," the boy yells. "Your punishment will be grave."

I don't know what to do as I watch them struggle, so I just stand there as she yells for me to help her. I watch as this spirit pulls her into the shower, and as she disappears I notice something forming on the bathroom floor. When Debbie finally vanishes, I see a young girl is sitting on the floor of the shower looking scared.

Before I can do anything, the spirit reappears and in a happy voice replies, "thank you for all your help, Carol. I'll never forget you or your sisters and all the help you gave me to defeat them. Thank you. Now go be with your mom and dad."

"I'll never forget you either. Thank you, Peter," Carol smiles.

The spirit disappears out of sight, and Carol stands up.

Perry Pankratz

"You're Carol?" I ask, shocked by what just happened.

"Yes. Peter just sent me back to be with my family."

"Come with me, Carol. I think you're going to make several people happy. Let's go see your mom, dad, and sisters," I reply, grabbing her hand just as my comrades break the door down.

"What the hell was going on here...is that Carol?" The sergeant asks, looking puzzled.

"Yes, this is Carol," I reply, watching her smile at them.

"Where's Mrs. Johnson?" He asks, looking around the bathroom.

"That is something I think we should discuss with a psychiatrist, sir. You would think I am crazy if I told you," I reply, shaking my head.

We walk out into the hallway, and as soon as Carol sees her mother, she screams out, "MOM!"

They all turn and look, surprised, and come running towards Carol. The girl lets go of my hand and runs to meet them in an embrace. I cannot help to tear up myself, watching them all together again.

Epilogue

By the end of July 1999, the Happy Hotel on 22nd Street closed down for renovations. A plaque was erected for Ms. Amanda Jay in the lobby for going far and above what any employee is expected to. This recognition came from the events of June 5-7th, 1999, where it was learned that she did indeed sacrifice her life for four children: Denise, Emma, Amy and Carol Fern. A note left in Carol's hand reads:

Dear friends and family, don't cry for me. I willingly stayed behind with Nightmare. His real name is Alex Bilard, and he is an amazing person. He did ask for these children's help, and in doing so he has stopped a far greater crime… the demise of humankind. I hope the parents of these children understand they have four special girls and although I only spent a short while getting to know Carol, she has managed to etch her way into my heart as well. I love you all. Edna, I loved getting to know about you and your life, and when we do meet again I have a tale for you! I don't have much time to get everything down as we are near the portal to the shower. I will say this, don't worry about Debbie Johnson either. Her husband is waiting for her return. Kisses to you all from the afterlife

xoxoxo

Amanda Jay.

Perry Pankratz
Synopsis

Good and evil - a battle that's been fought since the dawn of time. Both preying on the souls of humanity for the right to rule. After countless eons of this fighting, both sides come together for a mutual meeting. One that will turn humanity upside down. After forging an agreement between them, living people only learn what horrors await them on the other side once they pass through the arches of Helleven: a utopia for the ones who rule, and a nightmare for those who learn too late what becomes of them there.